Lock Down Publications and Ca$h
Presents

I0658210

CONFESSIONS OF A HITMAN

Love & Money

Written By
NICHOLAS LOCK

First Edition 2024

Printed in the United States of America

This is a work of fiction. Names, characters, places, and incidents either are products of the author's imagination or are used fictitiously. Any similarity to actual events or locales or persons, living or dead, is entirely coincidental.

Lock Down Publications
P.O. Box 944
Stockbridge, GA 30281
www.lockdownpublications.com

Like our page on Facebook: Lock Down Publications
www.facebook.com/lockdownpublications.ldp

Stay Connected with Us!

Text **LOCKDOWN** to 22828 to stay up-to-date with new releases, sneak peaks, contests and more…

Like our page on Facebook:
Lock Down Publications

Join Lock Down Publications/The New Era Reading Group

Visit our website:
www.lockdownpublications.com

Follow us on Instagram:
Lock Down Publications

Email Us: We want to hear from you!

SHOUT-OUTS

None of this would be possible without God giving me this talent.

Shout-outs to Cash and the entire Lockdown start for all the hard work that they do.

To everyone who supported me. I appreciate you and know that the best is yet to come!

First I have to thank God for this talent of playing with these words.

My fans, young and old, I appreciate you.

This is book number eight so I've shown love to everybody that deserved it. If you're not mentioned, then there's a reason!

Chapter 1

"Please, man! Please! I'll pay him! I just need a few more days," the man pleaded.

Dolo looked down over his shoulder and chuckled. Then he went back to heating the spoons up.

Dolo's 6'0" witty frame looked menacing to the man who was strapped to the chair. Dolo had been torturing Terry for the last three hours, bringing him to the point of losing consciousness, then injecting them with shot of morphine. Terry had made the mistake of getting twenty bricks of *girl* on consignment, fucking up the money. So Dolo had been called in, and for the hundred thousand he was getting paid he was more than willing to go the extra mile. Dolo fed off fucking shit up. He loved watching the light fade out of his victims' eyes.

"Man, please!" Terry begged when Dolo turned around holding the flaming hot spoon.

"Too late for *please*, my friend." Dolo held Terry's face down and used the hot spoon to pluck out one of his eyes.

The sizzle of hot steel burning Terry's skin brought a grin to Dolo's face. Dolo walked over to the kitchen window and opened it. The smell of burnt flesh was rancid. Rolling one of Terry's eyeballs in his palm, Dolo pulled his gun out and shot Terry in the forehead. Dolo took a picture of his handiwork and sent it to Jigga so that he would know that it was done. Dolo's dark-brown skin was glistening with the heat, beads of sweat lining his bald head. He wiped his head and pulled his gray toboggan down over his ears and stepped out of Terry's backdoor and into the brisk December night. Dolo walked around the house and eased his 190-pound frame into his black-on-black Camaro with the Batman symbol on the back windows. Dolo had come a long way in life. He'd had to scrap and claw his way up out of the slums. His rearing hadn't been one of the best. Then Dolo found some good news. Something he got a thrill out of: *killing*. Dolo could still remember his first kill . . .

Dolo was eleven years old, running around in the back of Campbell Terrace before they tore it down, when it was really the projects, enjoying himself. An old fiend had grabbed his arm, surprising him. Instantly, Dolo produced the kitchen knife he always carried around and stuck it into the old man's chest. Dolo jumped back, realizing what he had just done but quickly regained his composure. Dolo grabbed the knife and pulled it out, watching the fiend hold his chest and slide down the wall, leaving a crimson smear. Jigga, who was older at the time, came around the corner and saw Dolo standing over the dead fiend with a bloody knife. Initially, Jigga was thinking some crazy shit, but seeing the look that Dolo's face held, Jigga could see that he was to the good.

"You good, boy?" Jigga asked Dolo anyway.

"Yea," he said in a squeaky voice. The voice of a boy who had not gone through puberty yet.

Jigga got the knife and walked Dolo home to his mama. Dolo looked down at this phone vibrating in the console.

"What is it?" Dolo asked.

"Baby, I wanna see you," the feminine voice whined on the other end of the phone.

"Where you at, Candy?"

"In your favorite position," she purred.

Dolo grabbed his food and drove off. He had to go collect his money from Jigga, then he was going to swing by Candy's to blow her back out. It was Wednesday, so Dolo drove out to Stedman, a small town outside of Fayetteville, to Shannon's. Every Wednesday, Jigga would go to Shannon's, a little kickback joint that offered everything from ribs to pussy. She even sold legitimate lottery tickets! Whatever your heart desired, you could get. Dolo exited the car, eating the last of his nuggets, as two men walked out of Shannon's.

"What's it hitting on?" Dolo nodded towards Shannon's.

"The usual fast money, fast woman and slow niggas," one of the men responded, grinning.

Dolo walked up to the spot and rang the doorbell. The kickbacks was nothing more than a big two-story house that sat in a big field you had to drive two miles to get to it. Shannon never worried about getting robbed because there was another house close by that held a house full of her backup security. So, before you made it all the way, they'd be there waiting on you. To say Shannon made a lot of money would be an understatement. Sambo, one of the security guards, opened the door and let Dolo in upon seeing it was him. Dolo gave Sambo a nod and walked over to the bar.

"Let me get a bottle of water," Dolo told the bartender and turned to survey the spot.

Everything was the same as usual except that Jigga wasn't in his normal spot at the poker table. The poker table was packed, the dance floor was lit, and niggas and bitches were coming in and out of the back. There were three bedrooms on the first floor in the back that Shannon ran hoes out of.

Dolo threw the water back and started walking upstairs; very few were allowed upstairs. The office was located upstairs along with four other rooms, one of which was where Shannon held the high-stakes poker games. The other two were bedrooms, and that's exactly where Jigga was. Jigga and Melissa, who was Shannon's daughter, had a thing going.

"Come here, Sean," Shannon called out to him as he walked past her office.

"What I tell you about that, Ms. Shannon?" Dolo questioned.

"What?" She feigned ignorance. "And what I tell you about that *Ms. Shannon* nonsense."

She was the only one other than his grandma who called him by his government name. Everyone else was relegated to calling him Dolo. Dolo went by the name *Dolo* because anytime you saw him, he was nine times out of ten by himself. Jigga was the one who initially gave him the name. And Ms. Shannon told him to just call her Shannon; she had been around Dolo since he was a boy. Jigga's mom, and Dolo's mom used to be tight. Back in the day they were inseparable, but over time they had grown apart

"What do you want, Shannon? I got things to handle."

"Well, Jigga is in there with Melissa and he said he didn't want to be bothered," she relayed the message.

"Okay," Dolo said and walked out of her office, heading back towards Melissa's room.

Knock! Knock! Dolo knocked on the bedroom door.

"What is it?" Jigga's deep voice carried through the door.

"Nigga, you knew I was coming! Come on, so I can go!" Dolo started to get mad.

Dolo heard movement on the other side of the door. Then, it opened, and Melissa stood there in all her naked glory. Melissa was 5'6", 140 pounds with perky set of C cups. Dolo's eyes traveled down the patch of hair between her legs and back up. A sheen covered Melissa's golden brown skin. Dolo looked her in her hazel colored eyes and said, "Move."

"You could say *please*, boy!" She mushed Dolo in the side of the head as he walked past her. Melissa and Dolo had known each other since they were in diapers. They had been each other's first everything. They were just too much alike to be in a relationship. Dolo walked over to Jigga who was sitting on the bed with his back up against the headboard.

Jigga's small frame looked even smaller sitting in the middle of the king-sized bed. Jigga was only 5'4" and was 150 pounds soaking wet. His high-yellow complexion and green eyes made people assume he was a pretty boy, but he was as rugged as they come. He was little in stature but his name held more weight in the streets of North Carolina than a family of humpback whales. Jigga was a notorious jackboy back in the day but then he hit a lick for twenty bricks of cocaine and switched careers.

"You just couldn't wait," Jigga's deep voice rattled. He had one of those deep Barry White voices.

"The last time I waited on a payment, I didn't get paid," Dolo said, gritting his teeth. He was still upset about it.

"Not the big bad Dolo," Jigga joked. "You let somebody beat you out of your money." Jigga laughed, getting up.

"He's dead," Dolo stated blandly and tossed the McDonalds bag to him. Jigga loved the Big Mack with no mac sauce and extra mayo.

"I gotta hear this story one day." Jigga tossed Dolo three stacks of money.

"Do I gotta count this?" Dolo raised a brow.

"Get out, nigga!" Jigga smirked

Dolo walked out and sat in his car to count the money. Once he was sure it was all there, he drove off and headed home. Candy would have to wait until tomorrow.

Chapter 2

"Get your ass out here right now, Sean!" his mother yelled.

"Yes, mama."

"Why the fuck did you eat all of my candy?"

"There was nothing else to eat." He came down the project steps.

"Bring your little ass on here," Dolo's mother grabbed him by the shirt and dropped him in the kitchen. She opened the refrigerator and saw that the only thing in it was a box of baking soda and a few dead roaches. Instead of his mom admitting that she was wrong, she continued her verbal assault on eight-year-old Dolo.

"Well, your black ass shouldn't have eaten up all the food!" she yelled and turned around.

"But I didn't!"

Smack! She backhanded him to the floor.

"You better watch your damn mouth! Don't make me call the boogey man over here tonight!" she threatened.

"No, mama!" He started to cry.

"Stop fucking crying before I give you something to cry about," she warned. "Go clean your room now." He took off to go clean his already spotless room. The boogeyman that his mom was referring to wasn't the one that lived under the bed or the closet. He was the one that molested little kids. In reality, the boogey man was a local dope boy who preyed on the kids of his customers—who either ran up a debt and couldn't pay or outright trade their children for their fix—and what made it so bad was that he was only nineteen years old. Dolo dozed off while cleaning his already clean room. Presently, he sat up on his bed, rubbed the sleep out of his eyes and looked towards his bedroom door and saw the boogeyman standing there.

"No, no, noo!" Dolo woke up drenched in sweat. *It was only a nightmare*, he thought to himself, balling his fist. Dolo swung his legs on the heated tiled floor. He looked over at his clock and it read 6:30 in the morning. Dolo hated having dreams about his early childhood. It always left him in a sour mood. He went to the kitchen and grabbed a bottle of water out of the subzero refrigerator. Dolo then padded over to the floor-to-ceiling window and looked out over his property. Dolo's childhood was one of every type of abuse you could imagine—from physical to mental. With his mom being a junky and a prostitute, her focus was never on Dolo. All she wanted to do was get higher. He learned early on about self-preservation, and love was a foreign language to him unless it was spoken by his grandmother. Dolo and his mom stayed in Campbell Terrace but his grandma stayed a few minutes down the road on B Street. Every chance he got, Dolo would go to his grandma's. Thinking of his grandma, Dolo realized he hadn't paid her a visit in about two weeks. She was in a country club-style home for the elderly, although she could still get around on her own. She just suffered from Alzheimer's, and Dolo wasn't able to care for her the way she needed. He made a mental note to go see her soon. Movement in the yard caught his attention. Dolo walked closer to the window and looked out into the massive yard. The motion sensors that Dolo had strategically scattered about the ten-acre property that he owned should've been going berserk because when Dolo looked, he saw his two chow chows chasing a deer. How the deer got over the six-foot-tall white brick fence that surrounded Dolo's property was a mystery to him, but unless the deer got back over it,

Sasha and Simba we're going to kill him. Dolo ran down the spiral steps and out his front door.

"Sasha! Simba! Come!" Dolo yelled to his guard dogs. His twin chows ambled up to him, wagging their curled tails. Dolo reached down to pat their heads, and came back with bloody hand letting him know about the wound on the deer.

"Where is it? Go get him!" Dolo commanded and the chow chows sprinted off with Dolo trying to keep up.

The dogs led Dolo to a patch of trees where the deer was lying on its side with its throat ripped out. Dolo could only shake his head because that's what they were trained for—to kill. Dolo went and got his Silverado and loaded the dead deer into the truck bed. Dolo drove deeper into his property and parked. The hardest part about being in the toe tag business was disposing the bodies. So Dolo had come up with his own solution; he had a homemade pond towards the back of his property. Then he went and bought six baby alligators and put them in the pond with a twelve-foot-high privacy fence around it. Now that they were full grown, all he had to do was throw a body in the water or at the edge, and it would be a feeding frenzy. Dolo unlatched the private fence and peeked in. He'd raised them from babies, but they were still wild animals, and would eat his ass too, so he was extra cautious. There were two six-foot-long gators basking in the sun; that left four unseen in the murky water, and one of them was a twelve foot monster that Dolo called Godzilla. Dolo went to the truck and dropped the deer into the fence. He looked back and saw Simba and Sasha were sitting outside the fence.

"Pussies," Dolo said. Sasha and Simba wouldn't venture into the gator pen ever since Godzilla had tried to eat them when they were puppies. Once the two gators saw Dolo dragging the deer, they splashed into the water and started swimming to the side he was on. Dolo backed up and watched them drag the deer into the water. Godzilla surfaced and bit the deer in two as Dolo turned and left. That was only a snack.

***

"Man, what is it with you and big mac's with no mac sauce? Without the mac sauce, it's not a big mac; it's only a double cheeseburger," Dolo said to Jigga.

"I don't know. I just don't like the sauce. Listen, Dolo, I have a huge contract for you. The payout is colossal, the biggest one yet."

"How much?" Dolo's interest piqued.

"Ten mill."

Ten million dollars was a lot of bread. To this day the most Dolo had ever gotten paid was two million, and that had been to kill a drug lord in Georgia for a rival drug lord.

"Who do I have to kill and what are the stipulations?"

"Just a local girl." Jigga gave Dolo a picture of a pretty coffee-colored girl.

"The only stipulation is that you have to bring me her newborn, and Dolo, you cannot fuck this up," he warned.

"I've yet to fuck up and I'm not going to start now but what's the big deal about this one in particular?" Dolo nodded and left Jigga's mansion; he had an easy ten million dollars to earn.

Chapter 3

This was going to be Dolo's easiest kill ever, and the irony of it was that it was going to be his biggest payday. In his mind Dolo already knew how he was going to kill the woman. Dolo had been scoping her house out since he'd gotten the info on her from Jigga. Dolo knew she worked from 8 a.m. to 4 p.m. at the health department, and that her best friend watched her six-month-old daughter while she was at work. This made Dolo feel it would be easier. She'd be tired from a long day's work, then she'd have to contend with an infant. Then, by 10:30 at night, she would be in the bedroom getting ready to go to bed.

It was 10:55 at night, and Dolo was sitting on the porch in the woman's backyard. He'd waited until all the lights went out at her neighbor's house, then made his way to the back door. Dolo had already made sure that she didn't have an alarm system; the ADT signs in her yard were a scare tactic. He pulled out his lock pick set and went to work. No matter the lock, Dolo could get into anything at all unless it was a bank-style vault, and with time, he was confident he could pick that too. Basic deadbolts and house locks were a walk in the park. Dolo had the door opened in two minutes. He stepped inside the house, let his eyes adjust to the dark, then took in the layout. He was standing in the kitchen which led to the living room. He navigated the dark house as if he'd been living there since birth. Dolo stepped over a teething ring in the living room and walked down the hallway. He crept down the side of the wall on the balls on his feet. The first room he came to was empty save for a bunch of black trash bags. Dolo came upon the bathroom next, which was also empty. The only room left was the master bedroom. With the house being pitch-black, Dolo was able to move into the room without worry of being seen. He surveyed the room from the wall. There was a dresser without the mirror, a crib, and an air mattress which held the woman. Dolo pulled a Taurus .380 out and took its safety off. Dolo had gone over in his head how he was going to kill the woman while sitting on her back porch. Dolo walked on the balls of his feet until he got to the edge of the air mattress. Dolo pointed the gun at her head, getting ready to pull the trigger when the baby started to cry, startling Dolo. He had, for the most part, forgotten about the baby. Without opening her eyes, the woman grabbed the baby from beside her and put her to the breast. The baby immediately latched on and started drinking her fill. Dolo moved back to the edge of the bed and pointed the gun again. Finger on the trigger, Dolo and the baby locked eyes. He couldn't do it; he couldn't bring himself to kill the woman while she fed her daughter. Dolo quickly exited the house and got in his car.

He called Candy. "What are you doing?"

"Sleeping. What's wrong with you?" She could hear the frustration in his voice.

"Nothing. I'm on the way over there. Have the door unlocked," Dolo said and hung up.

Dolo and Candy's relationship—if you wanted to call it that—was strange, for lack of a better word. They weren't together, but they did all the things that couples did. As far as Dolo was concerned, the things they did were just something to do, but to Candy, they were everything. Dolo and Candy had met three years ago when she had run into the back of Dolo's car. Dolo initially had been steaming hot but when Candy got out of her car, his entire demeanor had changed. Candy was 5'9",185 pounds with fire-red hair. Her thick hair fell to the middle of her back, but on this particular day, she had two braids in. Candy had the build of Megan Thee Stallion, only her ass was bigger. Her ass put most black girls to shame. Candy's real name was Candace, but Dolo called her Candy because he reminded him of a candy cane, plus she tasted like candy.

When she got out of the car, Dolo told himself that he had to have her. They clicked instantly, and the rest was history.

Dolo pulled up outside of Candy's house and stepped out. He walked right into the house. Dolo kicked his shoes off and made his way down the wall. He was still in his bag about freezing up, but he had planned on taking his frustrations out between Candy's legs. Dolo walked into Candy's bedroom and saw her sprawled across the bed in a light-blue nightgown, snoring lightly. He stripped naked and walked to the head of the bed. He ran the head of his already hard dick across Candy's lips, causing her to open her purple eyes. She reached out, grabbed Dolo by the base of his wood, and put him in her mouth. The warm suction of her mouth made Dolo dig his toes into the carpet. Dolo grabbed her by the back of the head and let her mouth take away his frustrations. Candy relaxed her throat so she could take him all the way down her throat, and began to massage Dolo's balls.

"Mmhmmm!" Dolo gritted his teeth.

Candy felt him tensing up, so she knew Dolo was on the verge of climaxing. She started pulling back until the head almost came out of her mouth, then she would throw her head forward as fast as she could.

"Aahh!" Dolo released inside Candy's throat and fell over on the bed on top of Candy.

"Move, fucker! Get off of me!" She pushed him over. "And what the fuck is wrong with you?" Candy's face was as red as her hair.

"What you mean?" Dolo faked ignorance.

"Don't play with me!" Candy mushed Dolo in the side of the head.

Candy had been dealing with Dolo long enough to know his moods and how he acted. So she knew something had him in a funk.

"I just got a lot going on right now." Dolo rolled over onto his back and put his hands behind his head.

"You want to talk about it?" she asked sincerely, and he shook his head.

"All I need you to do is help me release some stress. The rest will take care of itself."

Candy grinned because she knew exactly what he wanted and needed. She pulled her nightgown over her head, straddled Dolo and rode him to sleep.

Chapter 4

It had been a few days since Dolo had backed out of his mission to kill the girl and kidnap her child but now he was back. Dolo was parked two houses down watching her house waiting for the light to go out, hoping this time would go nothing like the last time. Dolo was checking the clip on his Sig Sauer when two Suburbans pulled up outside of the house he was set to enter. Immediately, Dolo's antennae went up. Something didn't seem right. Dolo crunk the Challenger up that he'd stolen from the airport parking lot in case he needed to make a hasty exit. Five figures, dressed in all-black and carrying AK's, exited the SUV's, cutting off Dolo's train of thought.

Dolo opened his door and crouched down beside his car. He peeked around the front fender and saw them progressing towards his victim's house. Not wanting to leave anything to chance, Dolo came out of his crouch, firing his pistol. *Boc! Boc! Boc! Boc!* Two of them turned in Dolo's direction, leveling their AK's. *Kah! Kah! Kah!* The 7.62's coming out of the choppas could take a limb off. Dolo quickly ducked down behind his car and duck-walked to the back. He snuck a glance around the back and was met with more choppa rounds. Dolo dropped to his stomach and looked around the car. He saw the legs of the two choppa wielders and let off five quick shots. Both gunmen dropped to the ground holding their shattered shins.

Dolo ran around the car, put a bullet in each one of their heads and continued into the house. After all the noise the miniature gun fight had just made, Dolo knew time was something he had little of. He wasn't trying to let someone else collect the bounty on the chick's head. He dashed into the house and down the corridor. When Dolo got to the room the girl was in, he saw the remaining two assailants. One had the girl in front of him as a shield with only half of his face showing and the other one had his rifle trained on the sleeping baby but he also had a phone directed at Dolo.

"You see him?" the one holding the phone asked. Dolo dropped to a sitting position, letting his Sig bark on the way to the ground. The top of the head on the gunman holding the phone blew off, and the one holding the girl dropped to his knees with half his face gone.

"Aahh! Aahh!" the girl screamed and grabbed her baby. Dolo grabbed the phone to see who the man had been talking to but the call had ended, then Dolo looked up.

The girl and her baby were gone.

"Fuck!" Dolo ran through the house looking for the two, knowing they couldn't have gotten far.

Dolo ran outside as the first police cruiser came into view. Dolo reached down and grabbed an AK-47 from one of the dead men and started shooting in the direction of the cop. The cop immediately hit his brakes and started reversing down the street. Still no sign of the girl or her child. Dolo was once again forced to leave without securing his payday. What was more concerning to Dolo was: Who the hell were the armed men? Who had sent them? And who had been on the other end of this video call? And he knew just the person to talk to.

**

"Who the fuck did you give my contract to? And who the fuck is this bitch?" Dolo angrily asked Jigga.

"I didn't give the contact to anybody, and calm the fuck down!" Jigga matched Dolo's energy. "Here, drink some of this." He reached in the mini fridge and tossed Dolo a can of Heineken, but Dolo returned the beer, turning it down.

They were seated in the office of Jigga's soul food restaurant called Soul City. Jigga had taken some of his money and invested it into a local soul food restaurant and turned it into the go-to spot in Fayetteville. Jigga took one spot and turned it into four. You would think that the restaurant was frequented by mainly black people, but white people were the restaurant's main patrons.

"You know I don't drink." Dolo sat the beer down.

"Now you neglected to answer my last question. Who is this bitch? Because if you didn't give someone else my contract, then who were the five men I killed at her house?"

"Five men? What did they look like?" Jigga sat up in his chair.

"They had masks on but they had accents that I really couldn't place."

Jigga whistled, leaned back in this chair and put his hands on his head.

"This is all I know. I got a phone call and all they said was who they wanted killed, the stipulations and how much they were willing to pay. But if what you say is true, and I don't doubt it," Jigga quickly said, seeing the look that passed across Dolo's face, "then this is a situation in itself."

"And how is that?"

"Didn't you kill five men of unknown origin? So that means either I wasn't trusted enough to find someone to carry out the task or we weren't fast enough for their liking. Either way, I don't like it, not to mention the possibility of missing out on that payday but . . ." Jigga shrugged.

"As I was leaving, I saw the police putting the chick in the back of a police cruiser. When they get through with her, I'll be there waiting." Dolo stood up.

"What are you about to do?" questioned Jigga.

Dolo chuckled and said, "Do what I do best."

Dolo left the restaurant, thinking of what Jigga would've said if he had told him that, before he killed the armed men, they had been on a video call recording him.

Chapter 5

Geraldine Mallory lived in Heavenly Comforts, a country club-like rest home. They boasted numerous tennis courts, basketball courts, a lake, and an in-ground pool inside and out. There wasn't much the ten-acre compound did not have. Heavenly Comforts was broken up into two sections. On one side, you had the elderly people who still cared for themselves; they just needed help with minor things. Then, the other side had the elderly people who needed constant care, such as Mrs. Geraldine Mallory, suffering from debilitating illnesses.

Dolo's grandmother suffered from Alzheimer's; she'd only been there for the last year. Up until then, Dolo had hired a home healthcare nurse to come by and take care of her, but then her condition began to worsen, forcing Dolo to put her in Heavenly Comforts.

Dolo pulled the collar of his Prada sweater as he walked into the rest home. He kicked some of the snow off of his Prada boots and walked to the check-in desk.

"Hi, Mr. Mallory!" The receptionist beamed. "I haven't seen you in quite a while."

"Work has been having me with little to no time for anything else," Dolo replied.

"You can never have enough medical supplies," she added. Everyone was under the impression that Dolo sold medical supplies to hospitals and private companies for a big pharmaceutical company.

Dolo nodded, grabbed the visitor's pass with his name on it, and headed off to see his grandma. Dolo snuck glances in different rooms as he made his way down the corridor. In Dolo's line of work, some of those habits kept him alive. Dolo could think of quite a few people who would love to see his name on a tombstone.

"Well, look who it is, Ms. Mallory," the aide helping Dolo's grandmother said, seeing him in the doorway.

She turned and looked, and her eyes lit up, letting Dolo know that today was a good day for her. On days when her eyes were cloudy and had a faraway look, Dolo knew she wasn't herself. He hated those days because it was on those days that she barely recognized him, and it hurt him to the core.

"Hey, baby!" she shouted and fast-walked over to Dolo, wrapping him in a hug.

"Hey, Nah-Nah!" Dolo picked her up off the floor.

"Put me down, boy!" she squealed.

"How have you been?" he asked, and was about to take a seat on the bed.

"Oh no, rascal, you're about to take a walk with me. We can talk out there." She pulled Dolo up and out the door. Dolo allowed her to lead him outside. He felt like a little kid all over again.

"I've been well, what about you?" she inquired, looking up at Dolo.

At 6'2", Dolo towered over his grandmother's 5'0" form. She didn't look a day over forty years old. Her peanut butter-colored skin was almost wrinkle free. She had a full head of curly black hair with a few strands of gray here and there. To see her out and about, you would never guess her to be seventy-three, especially on days like today.

"I've been okay." Dolo looked around.

She slapped him in the back of the head. "Stop lying! You know I know when you're telling a lie. Something bothering you." She read him like a book.

Dolo weighed her statement. It was not like he was going to tell her that his mind was on killing a woman and kidnapping her daughter for ten million dollars, or the fact that whoever wanted her dead probably wanted him dead as well, since Dolo had killed some of his men.

"Just some stuff that I need to handle at work."

"Work? When are you going to get an honest job and stop doing the devil's work?" She glared at him defiantly.

"Nah-Nah, what are you talking about?" Dolo feigned ignorance

"Sean Darnell Mallory!" She stopped in her tracks. "Don't you dare look me in my face and act as if I'm not hip to what you do. I just don't say anything because you're a grown man now but know that I know"

"Okay, Nah-Nah," he smirked and they started back walking around the compound.

They walked for a while in silence. The only sound you could hear was the snow crunching under their feet. It was amazing to Dolo how Alzheimer's worked because right now, he had his grandmother back, but tomorrow she might not remember any of their conversation or who he was, for that matter.

"When are you going to meet you a nice young woman, have some kids and settle down?" she asked one of her regular questions.

"When I find someone worthy enough to hold the title of being Mrs. Mallory," Dolo said, but really had no intention of giving anybody his last name.

"Oh! Dang! I forgot! It's the first Wednesday of the month. I have a visitor coming."

"A visitor? Who?" Dolo wondered who could be coming to see her since he was her last living relative.

"That would be none of your business. Now give me a kiss before you go." She gave him her cheek.

"Before I go? Who said I was leaving?" Dolo asked, kissing her on the cheek.

"Stop being a baby. I told you I have a visitor that's coming to see me."

"Okay, I love you, Nah-Nah. I'll see you later," he said, thinking that she was on the cusp of going out. Dolo made sure she got back inside the building, and then he left. He had a date with a woman and her daughter.

Chapter 6

Dolo had been waiting down the street for the girl to come home for four hours, and hadn't seen a glimpse of her. But he wasn't going to move; he was very determined to kill her. Never before had a job taken this long or put him under this much stress. He was starting to take it personally.

"Yeah, what is it?" Dolo answered his phone.

"She's not coming home," Jigga said into his ear. "They have her under police protection."

"Police protection?"

"Yea. Things have gotten out of hand. We're gonna have to let this one go. I have another one lined up for you though," Jigga said dejectedly.

"Let it go? Nah, that ain't happening. I'm gonna kill this bitch and grab her daughter up like they want!" Dolo said assuredly.

"Maybe you didn't hear me. I forgot to mention this little fact—she's under federal protection."

"Federal protection? That doesn't make sense." Dolo stated racking his brain, trying to figure out why the Feds would get involved.

"Things are deeper than we originally thought. I got the rundown, but I can't tell you over the phone. You know where I'm at," he said and hung up.

Dolo took one more look at the girl's house and pulled out, heading towards Shannon's.

Shannon's spot was packed! The four inches of snow hadn't stopped people from coming out. Dolo was trying to figure out why the liquor house was so crowded, then he realized that it was Friday, and the first Friday of the month at that. Shannon was holding the high-stakes poker game tonight. Dolo found a spot away from everyone and parked. He sat there looking (through the tinted windows) around the big field that served as a parking lot. Dolo was looking for the jack boys because he knew that they couldn't rob Shannon's, but to catch a high roller going in would net them a hefty payday. Even though mostly everyone knew Dolo's get down, there were still plenty of people who would try their luck, given the right opportunity. Tonight was going to be a good night for whoever won because he spotted Bulldog's black CT-6 with the chrome lining, Milo's gray and black Range Rover Sport, Takesha's white Mercedes CLA AMG, and Rick's yellow Yukon. Every last one of them was playing with a big bank! Bulldog was a heavy hitter in the heroin game. Milo had a stronghold in the coke business. Rick was the old man, and Dolo didn't really know what Takesha did for a living. Dolo got out of his Silverado and made his way to the door. It was only then that he tucked his Glock .20.

"Came to take them down, didn't you?" Deebo asked, letting Dolo in. Dolo chuckled. "Might give them a chance at the title." The last time Dolo had played poker he'd left four hundred thousand dollars to the good.

It was crowded as hell inside the kickback, but it wasn't packed to the point where you were unable to move without bumping into someone. Dolo looked around the room and knew that trouble was brewing. TNT was in attendance and their sole purpose in life was to cause mischief and mayhem. Dolo himself had never had a run-in with the crew, but he was aware of their reputation. Then his eyes landed on Candy. Candy was looking like a whole meal. She had on a red Chanel one-piece that looked like she had gotten poured into it. Her figure was flawless! Dolo could see her pussy print from way across the room. The red one-piece accentuated her red hair. They locked eyes and she made a beeline towards Dolo.

"Hey, daddy," Candy purred, wrapping her arms around him and kissing him on the lips.

Dolo laughed while palming her soft ass. He knew the only reason she was acting extra was because of the excessive amount of women in the building.

"What's up, Candy?" Dolo buried his nose in her neck, losing himself in the scent.

"It's me and you tonight, right?" She rubbed his bald head.

"We'll see." Dolo broke their embrace and headed upstairs

'Uh-Uh! Where are you going?" she whined, grabbing his hand.

"To handle some business," he said with finality, and she let his hand go but not before kissing him again. Dolo walked up the stairs and went straight to the room where the high stakes poker games were held.

"Look who it is. Mr. Take-my-money-and-run," Milo said when Dolo walked in the room.

"Hope you came to give us a chance to get our money back," Rick added.

"Maybe." Dolo looked around the room

There was one seat left at the blue table. Ms. Shannon was in the far corner watching everything with the eyes of a hawk. Behind the bar was a dark-skinned beauty Dolo had never seen before. Bulldog's dark-skinned, husky body was seated beside the light-skinned Costa Rican Milo. Then beside him was Jigga, and brown-skinned Rick rocking a curly high top fade. Dolo took a seat beside Takesha's pretty caramel ass

"Scared money don't make no money," Bulldog smirked.

"How much do you need?" Shannon asked.

Dolo shook his head and said, "Let me get a hundred and fifty."

While she went to go get the money, Dolo looked at Melissa shuffling the cards.

"Long time no see," Takesha stated. "The last time I saw you, you hit me for almost two hundred racks."

"It be like that sometimes." He looked in her slanted eyes.

"Fuck all that, deal the cards!" Jigga said, impatiently.

"Lawball is the game," Melissa said, dealing the cards. Dolo already knew he was going to win. Melissa was an animal with some cards in her hand. And she and Dolo played with each other anytime they were on the table. Melissa knew some shit with the cards where she could set the deck and give you just about whatever cards she wanted you to have. That's why, almost every time Dolo played, he won. Then, he and Melissa would split the winnings. Dolo peeked at his five cards and had to keep the grin off his face. Dolo had six nothing off the deal.

"Check," Takesha said.

"Nah, checks came out on the first and fifteenth a thousand to bet." Dolo made the bet.

"*Boom!* The door flew off the hinges and in walked Ms. Shannon with a gun to her head followed by a bunch of TNT members and two dudes Dolo had never seen before.

"We can go about this one of two ways, easy or hard. All we came for is the money," said a tall brown-skinned nigga with a scar on his face. "Do you know where the fuck you at?" Rick had his face balled up.

Boc! Boc! The tall nigga shot Rick in the face, causing him to flip backwards out of his chair. He was obviously the one in charge.

"Everybody up!" a heavy-set light-skinned dude yelled. When Dolo stood up, he was going to draw down and shoot the one in charge, then the heavy-set nigga, but before he had a chance to, the tall dude said: "Whoa! Hold up!" He cast a glance at one of his goons and said: "Go get the gun off of him first."

He caught Dolo off guard.

"Yeah, I know who you are and your pedigree. This had nothing to do with you. In fact, I'm goin' to let you keep your bread. I'm gon' let y'all keep your money because we came for the house money. And before y'all try stalling us out, know that your security down the road has been taken care of!" said the tall brown-skinned nigga in charge, taking the air out of the room.

Dolo was fairly impressed because; whoever the nigga in charge was, he'd done his homework. He'd done the same thing Dolo would've done had he hit Shannon's. He'd also told Dolo that he didn't want any problems with Dolo without actually saying it. When it was all said and done, they hit Shannon for a mil.

Dolo found out that the reason the girl (whom Jigga had contracted him to kill) was in federal protection was because she was a federal witness in a case. It was starting to make sense to Dolo; that's why there was a contract on her head. But who was she a witness against? Dolo really didn't care; he'd gotten the address of the safe house from Jigga. So tomorrow, she'd be a memory.

Chapter 7

The safe house that the girl was being held in was located in Raleigh, the capital of North Carolina. Dolo had found out that the girl's name was Sade, and that she was only twenty years old, ten years younger than Dolo. The neighborhood that the feds had the safe house in was a gated community that you couldn't enter without the right sticker on your car. A few days ago, Dolo climbed the fence for some recon. He'd had on some jogging pants, a N.C. state thermal and running shoes. To anyone looking out of their window, he would've looked like someone out for a jog. Every house in the gated community had perfectly manicured lawns and foreign cars. Everything screamed luxury. This was the perfect place for a safe house, Dolo noticed. Anything that looked suspicious would, no doubt, garner a call to the police. Dolo had to figure out how he was going to get a vehicle in the gate, kill the woman and make it out with her baby in tow without getting into a high speed chase. At the moment, Dolo was parked down the road, contemplating his next move when it came to him as he watched a pest control truck ride by.

Dolo followed the pest control truck unit until it stopped at a gas station. Dolo parked beside the truck, got out and waited for the driver to come back out of the store.

As soon as the driver walked up to his truck and got ready to get in, Dolo hit him at the base of the neck with the edge of his palm, knocking him unconscious. Dolo easily picked the man up and put him in the trunk of his rental. Dolo secured his hands and feet, got the keys out of his pocket and closed the truck. Dolo searched the truck. He found an extra pest control shirt and put it on. Dolo didn't want to leave his car at the gas station, so he drove it across the street to the Wal-Mart, then walked back over and got in the pest control truck. This was going to be Dolo's way into the gated community.

"How may I help you?" the overweight guard at the security booth questioned.

"I'm here to set some rat traps at 171 Springfield Lane," Dolo recited the address he'd crammed.

"Okay," the guard nodded and hit a button, causing the gate to slide open.

Dolo had to smirk as he drove through the gate and made his way to the safe house.

Dolo parked the truck at the house next door and started checking the light-weight vest he had on. Dolo knew this was his last chance at killing Sade. If he did not succeed this time, it was going to be a done deal, so he came equipped with two Glock .30s with extra clips. Dolo wasn't aware of how many people they had guarding her, but at the moment, it didn't matter. A DISH Network van pulling up to the safe house drew his attention. An Arab stepped out and walked up to the door. Soon as the fed opened the door, the Arab shot him in the face, coating the front door with blood. The instant the shot went off, the back of the DISH Network van opened up and five Arabs in desert camo started hopping out.

"Man, damn!" Dolo yelled, cocking both of the Glocks. Judging by their look and the way they moved, Dolo could tell they were well-trained and meant business. Instead of trying to follow their lead, Dolo pulled the truck around to the street behind the safe house and got out. The Feds were going to try and get the girl to safety with the house under assault, and that's what Dolo was banking on. He hopped two fences and was in the backyard of the safe house. The inside of the safe house sounded like a war zone. Dolo high-stepped it out the back door and burst through it. Sade came rushing around the corner with her baby cradled in her arms and an FBI agent on her heels. Dolo and the fed both brought their guns up at the same time, simultaneously firing shots. Dolo's slug found a home in the forehead of the agent. At the same time, the agent's bullet caught Dolo in in the chest, knocking him back out the door onto his back. Dolo rolled over as an Arab came to the door.

Boc! Boc! Boc! Dolo shot him in the neck.

Dolo got up on his knees while grabbing his chest. His chest felt like a thousand needles were poking him. He looked around and saw Sade standing off to the side of the house. Dolo started making his way towards her. When he got close, she pulled a *snub nose* out and pointed it in his direction, making him stop in his tracks. She closed her eyes and pulled the trigger. Dolo closed his eyes, thinking that he let a nobody kill him, but he but didn't feel the impact of a bullet; then he heard a thump behind him. Dolo turned and saw a dead Arab behind him. Dolo turned back to Sade and they locked eyes. He made his way over to her and took her crying baby out of her arms. The instant Dolo grabbed her, she stopped crying.

"Come on," he said, leading her to the truck.

"Who are you?" she asked when they got in the pest control truck.

"None of that matters at this moment. All that matters is getting out of here safely and not going to jail," Dolo said, focusing on bringing them to safety.

Boom! The truck lurched forward.

Dolo looked in the rear view mirror and saw the DISH Network van preparing to ram them again. Dolo hit the gas, taking them through to open the gate. The van stayed on their bumper. Dolo checked one of the Glocks and passed it to Sade.

"If you want you and daughter to live, you'll take this and shoot." Dolo held the gun out to her while trying to focus on driving.

"I don't know what to do." She reluctantly took the gun.

"The same thing you did in the backyard. Only this time keep your eyes open and aim for the windshield." Dolo pulled his hand away from his chest and saw blood.

He needed to get to safety so he could see where he was bleeding from and how bad it was.

Sade laid her baby on the seat, leaned out the window and let the Glock speak. One of her rounds found home because the van swerved into oncoming traffic and hit an eighteen-wheeler head-on.

"Where's my gun?" Dolo questioned when he saw her hands were empty."

"I dropped it," she said innocently

Dolo shook his head and pulled into the Wal-Mart parking lot.

"You're bleeding," she said when they got inside the rental.

"I'll be okay," he said, pulling out and heading back towards Fayetteville.

They got to Fayetteville and switched cars. Dolo didn't know what he was thinking. His main focus at the moment was getting home to check his wound. In the entire ride, Dolo could feel her eyes on him. He couldn't focus on her; he needed to get home before he passed out. It was a welcome sight to see his gates. He hit the button to open the gates and drove to his front door. He stepped out with Sade on his heels. Dolo got the front door opened, and then he suddenly passed out due to pain and exhaustion.

Chapter 8

Dolo woke up in his bed with his chest wrapped in an Ace bandage. He looked to his right and saw Sade sitting in a chair with Simba's head in her lap while she stroked the pet's head, and Sasha lay at her feet. Then she had a gun (his gun, which she had found lying around) in her other hand. Dolo had to blink a few times because he couldn't believe what he was seeing. His chow chows didn't let anyone pet them.

"What are you doing?" Dolo croaked

"Waiting for you to get up," she said, matching his stare. "We have something we need to discuss."

"As in?"

"Why you keep popping up everywhere I am and why did you help me?"

"I have some questions myself." Dolo sat up and had to bite back a yell. The left side of his chest hurt to no end.

"Who's trying to kill you and why?"

"You first," she shot back.

"You're in no position to bargain. I saved your skin."

"As did I because the Arab that was behind you was about to send you to the afterlife. Plus, I'm the one with the gun and I'm the one who made sure you didn't bleed to death from that bullet wound!" she matched his tone.

That's why my chest is wrapped up, Dolo thought to himself. Nobody knew, but Dolo was a hemophiliac and could really bleed to death from an open wound.

Dolo was starting to think that he'd made a mistake bringing her to his house. She might not be as helpless as he originally thought. He debated on how much to tell her.

"I was supposed to kill you and kidnap your daughter," Dolo informed her. He didn't have anything to lose.

"So Abu hired an outsider to do his dirty work," she said to herself.

"Who is Abu?"

"That makes sense. Abu wouldn't have met you personally. He wouldn't want to further incriminate himself!" Sade said, continuing to talk to herself.

She looked at Dolo and shook her head. "You have no idea what you've gotten yourself into. First off, Abu is the prince of Saudi Arabia. When his dad, Talal, dies, he's set to become King of Saudi Arabia. Abu wants me dead because, first off, I know things about them that, if they get out, it'll hurt his country in the worst way. Second is because my daughter, Chadijah, is his firstborn, which gives her claim to the crown and until she becomes of age, I'll be the one in charge. I hope you've mastered your craft because you've put yourself in a bad situation." She walked to the huge picture window and stared.

"How so? I can still kill you and get this Abu character your daughter." Dolo stood up.

Sade looked at Dolo and laughed. "That night at my house when you killed them people, the one holding the phone that night was Amir. Abu's lieutenant and best friend. He's not going to rest until he has your skin, literally"

"What do you know that he wants you dead for?" Dolo needed to know how deep the well went.

"Only that he's funding ISIS and Al-Qaeda and selling drugs. And if the world, particularly the U.S., were to find out, then Saudi Arabia would be put in a situation of: either give Abu up or suffer the consequences. And I know for a fact that they won't give him up. I forgot to mention that his family owns eighty percent of the oil that comes out of Saudi

Arabia." She turned to look at Dolo to see if he understood how deep things went. "So it looks like you're stuck with me until this concludes."

What the fuck had Jigga gotten him into? The situation quickly got out of hand. It was nothing he couldn't handle, especially now that he knew what he's up against. Dolo grabbed his phone to call Jigga. He saw he had a bunch of missed calls from Heavenly Comforts. He called the rest home but didn't get an answer.

"Come on," Dolo urged, throwing some clothes on, forgetting the pain in his chest.

"Where are we going?" she asked, grabbing her sleeping baby.

"Just let's go." Dolo rushed out the door and went to his black Silverado.

Dolo sped off towards the rest home, hoping there wasn't anything wrong with his grandmother.

"What's going on?" Sade asked.

"I have to check on somebody," he said, fearing the worst. He pulled into Heavenly Comforts and got out. He fast-walked into the building, bypassing the sign-in desk, and went straight to his grandma's room.

"Hey, sugar," she said when Dolo walked in. Dolo released the breath he was holding. "Hey, Nah-Nah, what's been going on with you?"

"Mr. Mallory, we were trying to reach you yesterday," an aide said from behind him.

"What was wrong?" Dolo quickly questioned.

"Nothing now. We like to inform the family when something happens. Ms. Geraldine had a little fall and bumped her head."

"Oh, I'm okay. It was nothing. I don't know why they made a big fuss about it!" she protested. "Now come on, let's go for a walk." Dolo's grandmother grabbed his hand and led him out the room.

They were walking up the hallway when Dolo spotted Sade walking in their direction, carrying her baby.

"Oh my Lord! Sade baby, is that you?" His grandmother dropped his hand, walked up to Sade, and wrapped her in a bear hug.

Dolo had a bewildered look on his face as did Sade.

"Nah-Nah, how do you know her?" Dolo felt like she was about to have one of her episodes where she got confused as a result of her Alzheimer's.

"This is Sade. This is your baby sister."

Chapter 9

Dolo could remember it like it was yesterday. He was ten years old and his mom was pregnant. He was excited because it meant he was going to have a brother or sister to play with. But all that came crumbling down when she came home from the hospital with no baby. Whenever Dolo would ask where the baby was, he would get slapped to the floor.

After a while, he just stopped asking; he chucked it up as just another lie he'd been told.

"Um—hi," Sade said, looking from Dolo to his grandma.

"Oh, baby, it's so good to see you. How have you been? Whose baby do you have?"

"Mine and do I know you?" Sade had her face scrunched up.

"It's granny G," she said, and Sade's eyes got big.

"But—But—" Sade's words got stuck in her throat and her eyes got misty.

"What am I missing here?" asked Dolo.

"Poor baby, you never knew." His grandma looked at him. "Your mother signed her rights to Sade away at the hospital. She was barely taking care of you. She wouldn't have been able to take care of you both. Your mom signed Sade over to Ms. Linda. Linda couldn't have kids, so Sade was a blessing to her." She turned back to Sade. Where's Linda now?"

"She passed away two years ago." Sade wiped her face with the back of her hand.

"I kept in touch with Linda through the years but then she moved and we lost touch."

"I always wondered what happened to you." Sade wrapped her in a hug again.

"And this is your pretty baby?" She took Chadijah out of Sade's arms.

"Yes, that's my daughter—Chadijah," she beamed.

Dolo was sitting back, taking it all in. This put a whole new wrinkle in Dolo's game plan. With Sade being his baby sister, Abu was definitely the opp because he wasn't going to let anything happen to her. Dolo had gone from being her assailant to being her protector. But with all that, Sade had told him it was going to be a tall task keeping her out of harm's way. He needed to talk to Jigga asap. Dolo texted Jigga and told him that they needed to talk, and Jigga replied that he bet they did since there was now a bounty on Dolo's head for a hundred million dollars.

***

"I told you to leave it alone but you just wouldn't listen. Not only did you not kill her, but you earned yourself a tombstone beside hers!" Jigga paced back and forth.

"A tombstone? Picture that! Now if you're done talking out the side of your neck, I got something you need to know. Sade is my little sister."

Jigga sat on the edge of his desk, looking Dolo in the eye.

"You've really lost it. Your little sister? Dolo, you don't have a little sister!"

"You remember when I was ten and my mom was pregnant? She had her then but she gave her up at the hospital!" Dolo said with conviction.

"And what brought you to this conclusion?" Jigga asked, sitting down behind his desk.

"The instant my grandma saw her, she called her name and gave me a full rundown on her."

"I'll be damned. Your mom told me she was stillborn. Now you have to keep her alive." Jigga could only shake his head.

"Funny how the world works. Let me give you a refresher course on who it is that wants y'all dead. His name is Abu and he's as vile as they come. He has hands in everything, from the drug trade to human trafficking. Plus, he's a prince in Saudi Arabia, which makes him just about untouchable. The only person with more power is his father who is an honorable man. He has no idea what his son does behind his back!" Jigga said. "Well, let me rephrase that, he probably does know; he just turned a blind eye to it. The only way to get Abu off your ass would be to kill him, and you'd have a better chance at convincing Muslims that the pig is a clean animal."

"It's the solution to every problem," Dolo said.

"One more thing—you're going to have every killer in the world gunning for you—from petty killers to the real deal assassins. Come here, let me show you something"

Dolo walked behind Jigga's desk and looked at his computer screen.

"This is how I find your contracts. It's like an assassin network. People post who they want killed and how much they're going to pay. Only select individuals have access to this site, and the ones that do are about their business. Look at your picture, which I'm still wondering how they got that." Jigga pointed.

Dolo looked and saw a still frame of him the night he killed the men at Sade's house. Under his picture read a hundred million U.S. dollars and his last known location.

"No one really knows you're a major scale even though they should do. You're being looked at like a civilian who pissed off the wrong people. They'll be thinking that you're an easy hundred mil. The same way you thought Sade was going to be easy."

There is a huge difference between the two. I know how to shoot too," Dolo said arrogantly and walked out of Jigga's restaurant.

Winter was in full effect. Dolo couldn't think of the last time it had snowed so much in Fayetteville. The snow was about a foot deep. Dolo had to take a high step to get to his truck. He miscalculated one of his steps and stumbled to his knee, which saved his life. The instant he stumbled, the driver's side window on his truck shattered. Someone had taken a shot at him. Dolo rolled under the truck to the other side, trying to put something between him and the shooter. He wasn't sure where the shot had come from, but he was almost certain that it had come from behind him. Dolo opened the back door, and both windows shattered, but not before he was able to grab the AR-15 off the backseat. Being a sniper himself, Dolo knew there was only one logical place the shooter could be that would make more sense, and that was the roof of the YMCA across the street. Dolo had to get the shooter to give up their position, so he could get some shots off. Dolo crawled five cars over on his stomach so that he was to the right of the YMCA. He crawled under another truck and set his sights on the top of the YMCA. He grabbed his keys and hit the button to start his truck. Sure enough, the sniper started sending rounds through his windshield, giving his position atop the YMCA. Dolo sent three three-round burst into the sniper's location and waited. He peeked his head out and didn't get shot at. Either he'd spooked them or he'd hit them. Either way, Dolo wasn't going to stick around and find out, and wasn't in a good position to go back and forth. Dolo got to his bullet-riddled truck and drove home.

Jigga sent Dolo a text when he pulled into his driveway; it was only seven words. They read in capital letters: THE HUNTER HAS OFFICIALLY BECOME THE HUNTED.

Chapter 10

"I told you you were about to have your hand full," Sade said, sitting on the couch, feeding Chadijah.

Dolo had just woke up and really wasn't in the mood for her smart mouth. He forked a mouthful of the cheese eggs she had cooked into his mouth to keep from responding. Sade was going to take some getting used to because her mouth was crazy slick, but she got it honest. Their mom used to have a slick mouth as well. Dolo looked over at Sade and saw a young version of their mother. He didn't know how he had missed it to start with. She even had their mom's slim, but thick frame. However, instead of having their mom's dark-brown complexion, Sade was the color of coffee with a lot of cream in it. She also had the Mallory trademark: thick eyebrows and oval-shaped head.

"And you mean we're going to have *our* hands full because the way things are starting to look, I might need a little bit of assistance.

"I don't know how I could help you," said Sade.

"You'll see," Dolo stated, going to grab his ringing phone.

"Open this fucking gate!" Candy screamed into Dolo's ear. He looked at this security feed and saw Candy's red Challenger idling at his gate. He wanted to leave her ass out there because he'd told her not to pop up at his house without notice. He hung up and hit the button to open the gates. Dolo closed them back as he made his way to the front door. Candy parked at his front door and stormed up to him.

"Why the fuck haven't you called me?" Candy pushed Dolo in the chest, causing Sasha to go crazy.

"*House!*" Dolo pointed and Sasha padded in the house. "You're lucky she don't grab ahold of your ass. And I've been super busy, but you got shit confused because I don't have to check in with you." He put Candy in her place.

"Sean, I need to go grab some clothes," Sade said from behind him.

Since finding out that they were brother and sister, Sade had taken to calling him by his first name.

"Who the fuck is this bitch?" Candy glared at Sade.

"Get your whore in check, Sean," Sade warned.

"Your mama a whore!" Candy yelled, causing Sade to take off in Candy's direction.

Sade started punching Candy with a flurry of punches that would rival a professional boxer. Candy tried to get her shit together, but Sade wasn't letting up. Dolo wanted to break it up, but he had his reason for not stepping in. One was because, after all the things Sade had been through lately, he was sure she needed to let out some steam. Secondly, Dolo wanted to see what she was made of, and to confirm whether she had that fire in the veins. And so far she did. Candy had to outweigh her by at least fifty pounds and two inches but Sade's 5'7" ass was killing her. And lastly, Candy needed her ass whooped. Dolo stepped in when Candy's nose started bleeding

"Chill!" He grabbed Sade up.

"Let me go!" she screamed, struggling to get loose.

"No, it's over with. Candy, take your ass upstairs to my room and clean yourself up."

Candy shot daggers at Sade as she made her way into the house.

"I'll kill that bitch!" Sade spat when Dolo put her down.

"Calm down. It's bad enough that I allowed you to beat my little bitch up. Damn, what else you gon' do?"

"You better get her because next time I'mma kill that hoe." Sade walked back into the house. Dolo walked up the steps to his room to talk to Candy. He found her in his large bathroom at the dual sinks, cleaning her face. Dolo walked up behind her and placed his hands on her hips, looking at her through the wall mirror.

"Get your hands off of me," she said, but didn't move away from him.

"That's my little sister down here. If you would've took the time to ask instead of running off at the mouth, we wouldn't be here right now." Dolo walked over to the large walk-in shower and cut it on.

"Get in. I'll be back." He walked out of the room. Dolo found Sade downstairs in the living room watching Love and Hip Hop Atlanta. He grabbed Chadijah from Sade and sat her in his lap. She looked up at him and smiled, showing off her gums.

"Look, I'ma call my home girl and have her take you shopping. And let me ask you this. When are the Feds going to come looking for you and how much do they know?" Dolo inquired.

"They're looking for me right now and they don't know anything concrete yet. All they know is that I have damning evidence that Abu is helping terrorists, but I haven't given it to them yet."

"A'ight, we'll talk about it in-depth later on." Dolo called Melissa and she answered on the first ring.

"What do you want?" Melissa questioned.

"What makes you assume I want something? I might just be calling to check on your well-being."

"Yea, when hell freezes over, now what is it?"

"I need you to take my little sister shopping. Everything is on me, my treat."

"Okay. I was wondering when I was going to meet this mystery woman. My mom wanna meet her too."

"How do you even know? Never mind. I already know. And your mom is going to have to wait to meet her. Now, come on. I'm at my house."

"I'm on my way and my mom has something you need to handle regarding that night we got robbed," she said and hung up.

"I don't need a babysitter and I have my own money," Sade said smugly.

"Yes, you do and my homegirl's with the shit for real. And where you get some money?"

"I thought I told you I was messing with a billionaire. If you think my pockets didn't get laced, then you're little more foolish than I thought," she smirked.

"Look, my homegirl will be here in about twenty minutes. Let her in the gate and go handle your business. Do not get by your house or anything. And buy you a prepaid phone. I tossed your old one!" Dolo said, giving her his niece back and going back upstairs.

He was about to get some much needed sex because tonight he was going to hurt something.

Chapter 11

Tonight was Dolo's first time at Shannon's since the night it had gotten robbed. Ms. Shannon had improved her security tenfold since then. There were metal detectors at the entrance now, and the only way you got inside with a pistol now was: if you were on a list the bouncers had at the door. And that list wasn't really a list because the only name on it at the present time was Dolo's. The house down the road that her back up security was stationed, watching a live feed from Shannon's, now boasted three German Rottweilers. Shannon had also hired more security for the inside and outside as well. The only way to rob Shannon's now would have to be an inside job. Dolo felt like the only place safer was his house. Dolo had left Sade at his house where he knew she'd be safe until he got back.

"What is it that's so important, Shannon?" Dolo questioned impatiently. He'd been sitting idle for the last ten minutes.

"Don't rush me, boy. I am running a business," she said, not wanting to take her eyes off of the security videos.

"Ain't nobody gonna try you no more, relax!" he said.

"And I want to make sure of it." She got up from behind her desk, causing Dolo to take a quick breath.

Ms. Shannon was pushing sixty, but her body was like that of a twenty-five-year-old. Shannon was easily the thickest woman he'd ever seen in his life, and the white Gucci bodysuit she was wearing solidified it. Shannon couldn't have been no more than 5'5" with no stomach. Her reddish-brown skin was wrinkle-free and smooth. Her most appealing feature was her doe eyes that always had a seductive look. She patted her black bob with red streaks, as she sat down in front of Dolo. If she was aware of the effect she was having on Dolo, she didn't show it.

"I've been thinking about that night, and it's no way I should've been able to get robbed like that. I feel like it was an inside job and I know you can get to the bottom of it!" Shannon said, wearing a face that let Dolo know she meant business.

"Who do you suspect?"

"I don't know but if you haven't noticed, all the faces inside are new. All the old security guards are at the house down the road and that's where I want you to do your work"

"You do know what it is you're asking?" He had to make sure she knew what she was asking.

"I do and after you find out, if you find out, don't kill, save him for me. There'll be a quarter mil in it for you, and take Melissa with you!" she said before walking out of the room.

Dolo hadn't taken Melissa in to do dirt since she was twenty years old. Some tens of years ago. A lot of people didn't know that Melissa could get down and dirty. And she would do it willingly with a smile on her face at that. He could still remember the first time he and Melissa had gotten blood on their hands together . . .

"Don't freeze up on me," Dolo warned Melissa.

They were both sixteen years old and reckless beyond measure. They were on the outskirts of Fayetteville in a city called Raeford, aka Bucktown. Their sole mission was to send a message. If you hit one of Jigga's spots, the price to pay was death. Two brothers had hit a trap Jigga had on the west side and made off with fifty racks and a quarter bird. Dolo wasn't worried about being seen, so he parked the stolen Expedition in front of the house. It sounded like the people in the house were having party. Dolo and Melissa checked the 40's they were carrying and knocked on the door.

"What's up?" a tall dark-skinned dude with cornrows answered, smoking a blunt. He was the older brother.

"You." Dolo punched him, knocking him backwards into the house.

There were four people in the house, the two brothers and two girls, and they were all in the living room.

"What the fuck is this?" the other brother asked.

"Looks like a party to me," Dolo said, seeing the opened quarter brick on the table. "Tie their hands behind their backs," Dolo told Melissa, keeping his gun trained on them.

"Wait, we don't have anything to do with this," one of the girls said, earning her a slap from Melissa.

Once they were secured, Dolo and Melissa went to work! They cut their clothes off and chopped each of them into ten pieces. After they were done, they were covered in blood. Dolo was surprised that Melissa had not batted an eye through the whole ordeal.

"Don't freeze up," Melissa mocked Dolo.

"What are you talking about?" he asked, getting ready to walk out the door.,

Melissa walked up to him and kissed him in the mouth. They ended up fucking on the couch a few feet away from the mutilated bodies. They gave new meaning to the word *blood lust*. Every time they killed somebody, Melissa would want to fuck. This went on for four years, then Dolo stopped taking her with him.

Dolo snapped out of his walk-down-memory-lane and went to find Melissa. He found her at the bar taking shots.

"Come on," Dolo told her and she came without a smart remark. Shannon must've told her daughter beforehand what time it was.

"What's the plan?" she asked once they got in Dolo s Camaro

"Do we need one?"

"I guess not."

Since it was Melissa's mom that had gotten robbed, he was going to let her take the lead. They drove the short trip down the road to Shannon's back-up security house. Sambo let them in immediately after seeing Melissa. Dolo grabbed the automatic shotgun lying on the dining room table and cocked it, grabbing everyone's attention. There were five security guards in all.

"Now this is the situation we have," Melissa said while pulling a pair of black leather gloves down over her hands

"Us getting robbed was an inside job and I'm here to find out which one of you was in on it."

"What? Y'all got me fucked up!" Sambo started to get excited.

"Sit down, Sambo." Dolo trained the pump on him, and he did as he was told.

"Matter of fact—y'all take a seat!" Melissa said. After they sat down in the kitchen chairs, Melisa tied them all down.

"Now I hope all of you know this is business—nothing personal," she said, walking out of the house.

"Make it easy on me and yourselves and just confess," Dolo tried to give them a way out.

"We ain't have shit to do with it," Sambo spoke up again.

"Would you bet your life on it?" Dolo inquired and he got quiet.

Melissa wheeled a portable car battery charger in the house and sat down in front of Sambo. She cut the shirts off of all five of them and went into the kitchen. Dolo didn't know what kind of trick she was up to. She came back out, carrying a dripping wet knot, the type of whip that they used to beat Jesus with in *The Passion of the Christ*. Dolo took a seat on the couch because he knew Melissa was about to put on a show. She stopped in front of Brandon—a new guy on the security team. Melissa pulled back and slung the knot across Brandon's bare chest. *Crack!* It embedded itself in his skin, so when she pulled back, the skin came out.

"Ahhh!" he screamed in agony.

"Anybody wanna fess up?" she asked, smirking.

Dolo knew she didn't want a confession. She wanted to hurt something; she got off on hurting people more than he did. *Crack! Crack! Crack! Crack!* She gave each of them a taste of what was to come. The screams were irritating to Dolo.

"Hurry up, woman," Dolo said.

"I'ma kill you, bitch!" Sambo gritted his teeth.

"Is that a fact?" Melissa cocked her head to the side. She walked in front of Sambo and squatted down in front of him. She used a razor to cut the rest of his clothes off. Melissa grabbed the prongs to the battery charger and hooked them to Sambo's nuts.

"Now did you say *I'ma kill you, bitch*?" She smiled. "Wait, I'll tell you what. Just tell me which one of y'all it was and I swear I won't kill you but you'll have to leave the state!" she swore

"Okay, man, it was me!" Mitch spoke up. "Face paid me a hundred thousand to set it up," he confessed.

"Damn, you took all the fun out of it," Melissa said, hitting the switch on the battery charger.

Sambo jerked as the charger sent volts of electricity through his body. Dolo looked at Melissa and could see her nipples had gotten hard. She was horny. The charge was frying Sambo; he literally had smoke coming out of his ears. Dolo went into the kitchen and grabbed a spoon.

"Cut it off, he's dead!" Dolo said before calling Shannon. "It was Mitch—he confessed that someone named Face paid him to do it." After hanging up, he looked at Melissa. "She's on the way," he told Melissa. Dolo used the spoon to pluck Sambo's eyes out and put them in a bag.

"You still do that shit?" Melissa asked, walking up to Dolo.

"Yes and no," he said firmly.

"Now what?" She feigned innocence.

"I know that look, plus your mom's on the way."

"I won't take long. What has it been for ten years?" she asked, pulling her jeans off.

"I ain't fucking with you, woman."

"Fine! Jerod!" she called one of the security guard's name she cut the pants off of him. She squatted down in front of him and put his dick in her mouth. Once he got hard, she turned around and sat down on his dick. Melissa bucked her hips and pinched her nipples all the while staring Dolo in the eyes. Her body stiffened up as her orgasm washed over her.

"You fucked up," Dolo commented on the scene in front of him.

"I know," she said and cut Jerod's throat with the razor.

"I thought you weren't gonna kill me," Mitch sobbed.

"I'm not but she is," Melissa pointed at the door with Shannon standing in it.

"I'm out. I'll come by in ten in the morning to get the bodies," said Dolo.

Chapter 12

The sun had just peeked over the horizon when Dolo pulled into his driveway. The temperature said 25 but it felt like it was 10. He had just gotten back from picking up the bodies of the security guards at Shannon's; he hadn't fed the gators since the day Sasha and Simba had killed the deer, so he knew they were hungry. As Dolo was driving past the house, Sade stepped on the front porch.

"What are you doing up so early?" Dolo stopped and allowed her to get in.

"I couldn't sleep and I heard the motion sensors going off, so I went to the monitors and saw you coming up the driveway. But what are you doing up so early?" She flipped it back on him.

"I had to go get my pets some food," Dolo flashed a sarcastic grin.

"I fed Sasha and Simba when I got up."

"Those aren't my only pets," he grinned as he pulled up to the gator pen.

"What kind of pets do you have that require them being kept inside a privacy fence?" questioned Sade.

"You're about to see." He got out of the new Silverado he'd just bought and walked around to the back.

"Oh my God!" Sade gasped and put her hand over her mouth when Dolo pulled the tarp from over the truck bed.

Inside the truck bed were the bodyguards from Shannon's.

"Come on! Hurry up so you can help me."

"Help you what?"

Dolo just shook his head and started dragging the bodies off the truck. He was trying to hurry up because the thermal that Dolo was wearing wasn't doing anything to keep him warm. Dolo went to the privacy fence. He cracked the gate open and peeked in. All of the gators were in the murky water unseen. You could see the steam coming off of the pond. When Dolo was making the pond, he put thermal pads in different spots in the water, so that the water wouldn't freeze. Dolo grabbed the bodies and dragged them into the enclosure; he lined them up at the water's edge and backed up.

"What exactly is in that water?" Sade asked with her eyes squinted like she already knew the answer, but she wanted him to confirm it.

"You're about to see," he said, but none of the gators ever surfaced.

Dolo walked over to the water's edge and tapped the water with his foot. Immediately a gator lunged out of the water in his direction, causing Dolo to jump back and fall.

"Sean!" Sade screamed from behind him somewhere. Dolo scrambled back on his back from the fast-approaching gator. Then, Sasha and Simba appeared on each side of the gator, snarling and trying to take bites out of the gator. The gator snapped at the dogs, giving Dolo a chance to get up and run to the gate, followed by Sasha and Simba. Dolo looked back as the gators dragged the bodies into the water and tore them to pieces.

"You got some Lake Okeechobee shit going on, bro," Sade said, once they were seated inside the truck.

Dolo did not respond; he was still trying to catch his breath and calm his nerves. He'd almost ended up being gator food. He pulled up to his house and went straight to his man cave. Dolo went to the bar, opened a bottle of peach Cîroc and took a long swig. Dolo didn't drink, but he needed to calm his nerves. If you took a look at Dolo's bar, you wouldn't know that he didn't drink. He had a wall full of liquor, and none of them had ever been opened until now. Well, a bottle of 1942 was open, but that was only because Candy liked to drink it.

"This house is really big." Sade walked into his man cave.

"I designed it myself." Dolo took a seat on one of the chocolate couches.

Dolo had bought the ten acres that his house sat on for a huge discount. It was a regular house to him. There were six bedrooms, five and a half bathrooms, and a three-car garage. Dolo came from the projects, so he felt like he deserved to live in luxury. Dolo had a say in every stage of the building process. Everything was Dolo's idea, from the marble floors to the vaulted ceilings, even the wine cellar which led to a safe room that had a secret passage that led under Dolo's property to the neighbors' yard. Dolo had the white brick fence installed all the way around his property with cameras mounted every few feet. There were motion sensors on the wall. So, to approach from any direction would alert Dolo. The front gate appeared to be an ordinary gate, but it would take a tank to break through it. It was made of a material that, if rammed, it would give in a little and bounce back. The windows and doors to the house had four-inch steel plates that would come down at the press of a button, making the house an impenetrable fortress. Dolo had explained everything to Sade. He had a weapons room that the military would be envious of. There wasn't a gun that he didn't own.

"Now let me know something I can use to my advantage against him and what evidence do you have on him besides your word against his?" Dolo needed everything laid out on the table.

"I have a memory card that I downloaded all the files from his personal laptop to. It has everything, from who he pays to their group name, as well as the banks and routing numbers."

"Okay. That's perfect, but is there a way I can get to him? To kill him would alleviate the threat against our lives," said Dolo.

Sade only shook her head. "Everywhere he goes, there's always a boatload of his personal security with him and he rarely comes to the States unless . . ." she stopped.

"Unless what?"

"Something goes wrong with one of his businesses. He owns every Arab gas station on the east coast and also the BP gas stations. He has a fifty percent stake in the BP's." Sade gave Dolo a jewel.

Dolo whistled. There was a BP gas station on just about every corner, and if there wasn't a BP, then there was an Arab store there. If there was one thing a businessman hated, it was losing money. Dolo was about to see if he could assist Abu in the loss of some revenue.

Chapter 13

"Hold it like this and use the sight lines like I told you," Dolo instructed Sade.

They were at the gun range behind Jim's pawn shop. Dolo was trying to train Sade how to shoot. If Abu really had the connections they said he did, then he didn't need to be the only one that knew how to shoot. *Boc! Boc! Boc! Boc!* Sade emptied the clip into the target

"Let's see if you hit something." Dolo hit the button to bring the target to them. "Now this is how you shoot!" Sade had hit the target in the chest with all but two shots.

"Are we done now because my arms hurt?" Sade complained.

"And I'm ready to get back to my baby." They had left Chadijah in the care of Ms. Shannon and Melissa.

"Let's go, cry baby!" he grinned as she stuck her tongue at him. Sade had grown on Dolo the past few days. Their bond was strengthening by the day, and Chadijah had latched onto him. Anytime she saw him or heard his voice, she would cry until he would come pick her up. They climbed in Dolo's Camaro and peeled out.

"Have you given any thought as to how you're going to go at Abu?" asked Sade.

"Yea. I'ma start blowing his gas stations up one by one. Sooner or later, he'll get the message."

"And what message is that? Unless you plan on blowing a lot of them up at one time, you're only going to make him mad by costing him money."

"That's the plan because once he gets mad, he'll start getting reckless and hopefully he'll show himself."

"Or maybe he'll up the bounty on our heads. You might be better off doing something to his uncle."

"Who is his uncle and why didn't you say something about him days ago?"

"I forgot and his uncle is who runs his businesses over here in the US. I don't know how much you care, but he doesn't have anything to do with the illegal stuff Abu is involved in."

"Where can I find him?" Dolo could give two fucks if he was involved or not.

"His office is located in uptown Charlotte. I can show you."

"What the hell!" Dolo looked in the rearview mirror and saw blue lights on a black charger.

"I've been telling you about speeding," Sade chastised him.

Dolo pulled over and the cop pulled over behind him.

"Damn!" Dolo said when the sexy brown-skinned woman exited the unmarked car. "What seems to be the problem, officer?" Dolo smiled, letting his window down.

Boc! Boc! Boc! Skrrr! The woman started shooting into the car, and Dolo hit the gas so fast that the Camaro fishtailed. Dolo made sure Sade wasn't hit. Then he checked himself. The window not being rolled all the way down had saved them because it deflected the first shot. Had she waited a few more seconds, she would've had an easy kill shot.

"You good?" Dolo asked Sade.

"Yea, just get me to my baby."

They went and got Chadijah from Melissa and headed home. Dolo had just gotten a wake-up call; he realized now that he had to take Abu serious.

"So you're going to let him live?" Dolo asked Shannon, referring to the dude, Face, who had orchestrated the robbery.

"At first, I wasn't but it would cost me more to go back and forth with him," Shannon said, pouring herself a shot of Jose Cuervo.

They were at Shannon's in the office but it was empty. Everything was gone, even Melissa had taken off.

"Every battle is not worth fighting, Sean. Sometimes you have to cut your losses." She dropped some words of wisdom. "Your mother would've been proud of you."

"I doubt it. I used to feel like she hated me." Dolo sat back on the sofa.

"Baby, she just had a weird way of showing her love, but she definitely loved you. You are her only son, and I don't know what it is about mothers and their sons, but it's a strong bond." She came over and sat beside him.

"What makes you think she would've been proud?" questioned Dolo.

"Because she would always say you were gonna make something of yourself and get her out of the hood. Then you turned into a very handsome young man." She rubbed his head.

Dolo smiled. "And you turned into a very beautiful, thick woman." He stared at the gap between her legs.

"Is that right? I don't think I'm that thick. I've been thinking about getting a Brazilian butt lift." Shannon stood up in front of him.

Dolo looked at her standing in front of him with her legs popped back, making her already plump ass stick out. Dolo took a chance and grabbed her by the hips and pulled her down on his lap.

"Boy, what are you doing?" she asked him, but didn't make an effort to get up.

"Shh," Dolo whispered, then kissed her.

Dolo ran his hands under her dress and grabbed her phat ass. His fingers sank into her butt like a head on a feather pillow. Dolo stood up and she wrapped her legs around his waist. Dolo carried her down the hall to her room and closed the door behind him with his foot. He sat her on the edge of her dresser and stared at her. Shannon looked at Dolo with one of her brows raised and a look on her face, as if to say: *What now, nigga?* Dolo stepped back and got on his knees. He pushed her dress up, so that it was bunched around her waist, and kissed her on the clit.

"You know you're not supposed to play with your food," Shannon said and pulled Dolo's face between her legs.

"Sss!" she hissed when he sucked her clit into his mouth.

Dolo flicked his tongue back and forth across her sex button, causing her pussy to get wetter. He took two fingers and began to slide them in and out of her love tunnels while continuing to flick his tongue across her clit.

"You better eat this pussy, boy!" she yelled in ecstasy. Shannon threw her head back and started rocking her hips, getting lost in Dolo's oral talents. Dolo ran his tongue from her clit all the way down to her ass, where he stuck his tongue in her bootyhole.

"You nasty!" Shannon screamed. Dolo went back to Shannon's clit, where he drew eights with his tongue, sending Shannon over the edge. She coated Dolo's tongue and face with her love potion. Dolo stood up and stepped out of his Gucci jeans. He rubbed the head of his dick up and down Shannon's center, coating it with her wetness. Dolo entered Shannon and almost came; her box was so tight and wet that Dolo contemplated making her his wife. He pushed all the way in and paused; he had to get his bearings. There was no way he was going to embarrass himself and nut quick. Dolo put Shannon's legs over his shoulders and started long-stroking.

"Mmm! Mmm! Mmm!" she moaned.

Dolo pulled out and backed up.

"Why do you stop?"

"Come over here and bend over." Dolo had to hit her thick ass from the back.

Shannon walked over to the bed and got on all fours while looking back at him. Dolo shook his head because her ass was still wobbling and Shannon wasn't moving. He pushed one of her ass cheeks up while he used the other hand to guide himself into her dripping wet center.

"Fuck!" Dolo said as her wetness enveloped him.

Dolo started pushing all the way in and pulling all the way out, hard! Dolo was stroking her hard and fast.

"Sean! Sean! You fucking me sooo good!" Shannon moaned out, making him stroke harder.

Every time he would stroke her ass, it would move like it had water in it. Dolo felt the nut coming and sped his strokes all the way up. Knowing she couldn't get pregnant, Dolo sprayed her insides with his unborn seeds and collapsed on the bed.

"That's some of the best pussy I ever had," Dolo said, out of breath.

"Wait until I put this mouth on you," Shannon said. Putting his softening member in her mouth, Shannon sucked Dolo back to life, and they started round two.

Chapter 14

After the last attempt on his life, Dolo was ready to go on the offensive. Sade had told him everything she knew about Abu's uncle, Muhammed. Dolo was about to make sure Abu knew that he wasn't the only one who had power. Since Abu's uncle was the one who ran his business in the US, killing him would hopefully force Abu to come to the States.

Dolo was parked in uptown Charlotte in a rental. He wasn't going to drive any more of his cars until the situation was handled. Dolo wasn't going to make himself an easy target. Dolo watched the slanting snow fall to the ground while he waited for Muhammed to come out of his office. Dolo's plan was to follow him to his house and kill him. Sade didn't know where he stayed. All she knew was where his office was and the kind of car he drove, which was a dark blue Maserati MC20 with black rims. He didn't have to wait long. Muhammed walked out and got into his car. Muhammed was only about 5'7" and overweight. There was no denying that he was a foreigner; he had the whole Middle Easterner look. He had on full Muslim garb, full beard and a kufi. Dolo pulled out a few cars behind him. He followed Muhammed to the Southside of Charlotte, where he pulled into an apartment complex that looked like some high-rise condominiums. Dolo hurried up, parked and got out. Dolo was walking up just as Muhammed was exiting his Maserati. Before he had a chance to react, Dolo knocked him unconscious with the butt of his gun. Dolo laid him on the ground and went to Muhammed's Maserati. Dolo grabbed his laptop and briefcase, then went and pulled his rental over. Dolo put Muhammed in his truck and started the two-and-a-half-hours drive back to Fayetteville. Dolo was going off of his initial course of action. Before he killed him, Dolo was going to see what kind of intel he could pry out of him. An hour into the drive, Muhammed regained consciousness and started yelling inside the trunk. Dolo turned up the song that he was listening to, and pushed the speedometer to eight. He pulled into his driveway and around to the back of the house. Dolo pulled his gun out and popped the trunk.

"Get your ass out," Dolo said, aiming the Glock.

"What is going on? What is it? Money? You want money? I have plenty. All you have to do is take me to my house." Muhammed tried to bargain, not realizing that it had nothing to do with money.

"Get out! Last warning!" Dolo's next words were going to come out of the end of the Glock. Muhammed must have sensed his impending doom. So, he started climbing out the trunk. Dolo motioned to the back door with the Glock. Sasha and Simba appeared on each side of Muhammed, growling low in their throats. With them there, Dolo knew he could move more freely. He knew if Muhammed even breathed wrong, they would be on his ass. Dolo stepped in front of Muhammed, opened the back door, and led him down into the wine cellar. Dolo led him deep into the wine cellar and stopped. He reached behind one of the racks that held the wine and flipped a switch. The rack popped out, Dolo grabbed it and swung it out, revealing a short hallway. The short hallway led to another room.

"Oh no!" Muhammed groaned when they walked inside. The room they were standing in had jugs with eyeballs in them on two whole walls. Then on another wall there was a chain link fence nailed to it. Dolo stripped Muhammed down and tied him to the fence.

"What are you about to do to him?" questioned Sade as she walked in the room and saw the set-up. "And please tell me that these aren't human eyes."

"Sade, what's going on? What's the meaning of all this?" Muhammed asked. She shrugged innocently and nonchalantly said, "Some stuff Abu had goin' on. Oh my gosh! These are human eyes! Why do you have these and what are they in?"

"They're from a majority of the people I've killed and they're in pickle juice. It keeps them from decomposing. Now if you go back upstairs, I have work to do."

"No, I think I'll stay and watch." Sade went and stood behind Dolo. In front of Dolo was a table that held all types of weapons that he used to torture people. There were large shears, hammers, drills, knives of all kinds, but the main item on the table was a car battery with wires coming out of it that led to the fence.

"Muhammed, save yourself some pain and torment and give me the information I need. I want to know where Abu is."

"I don't know!"

Dolo put a leather strap in Muhammed's mouth and said, "It would be wise of you not to spit this out." Dolo didn't waste any time; he flipped the switch on the battery and sent electricity streaming into the fence.

"Aarrghh!" Muhammed groaned out, sweat covering his entire body.

"You were saying what now?" Dolo let the switch off.

"I don't have anything to do about Abu's dealings," he said, lying.

Dolo hit the switch again; this time he didn't bother with the leather strap.

"Rrr! Rrrr!" Muhammed growled and lost his bowels. He started urinating on himself, and Dolo heard a stifled laugh from Sade.

"Still don't know anything?"

"He's—He's in Syria meeting with a general in ISIS." Dolo looked over at Sade with a look that seemed to say: *I thought he doesn't know anything about Abu's illegal activities.*

"Now what you're going to do is tell Sade everything, and I mean everything, that there is to know about Abu. Sade, if you have any doubt in what he's telling you, then hit the switch for a few seconds."

"And where are you going?" she asked, seeing he was about to walk out of the room.

"Upstairs for a minute. You got it." Dolo kept walking.

Dolo went to the rental and popped the trunk. There, lying in the middle of the trunk, was Muhammed's phone. Dolo thought he had seen it earlier, but he'd been more concerned about getting Muhammed inside. Dolo thumbed through the phone, checking out Muhammed's contacts. He spotted Abu's name and put all the numbers under Abu's name inside of his phone. Dolo walked back in the house just as Chadijah began to cry. Dolo went to the room that he and Sade had converted into a baby room and picked her up. He went downstairs, warmed Chadijah a bottle up and fed her. Dolo burped her and changed her diaper as the howls from the cellar drifted up the stairs. He should've closed the door. Chadijah went back to sleep after ten minutes of cradling her. He put her back in the baby room, then went back in the cellar and found Muhammed with his head hanging on his chest, and Sade leaning over the table scribbling something on a piece of paper.

"What's the deal?" Dolo inquired, checking Muhammed's pulse.

"I got a boatload of information," she said excitedly. "He was reluctant at first, but after hitting the switch a few times, he told me everything I needed to know. And he was involved in Abu's nefarious activities."

Dolo was secretly proud of Sade. She had that Mallory blood running through her veins, after all.

"What kind of intel do you have that'll benefit us right now?"

"I have the password to his computer and it has the address to every BP and Arab store he owns. The address to all the real estate that Abu owns, the powerful people that they have in their pockets and it has Abu's schedule for the next six months!" Sade bragged.

"I guess it's a good thing that I grabbed his laptop then," Dolo smiled.

Dolo went and got his laptop, and Sade downloaded all the files to a memory card, so that they could have all the information that they needed. They tied Muhammed's hands and feet tightly, and walked him blindfolded into the gator pen. They pushed him into the water where they recorded the gators eating him alive. Losing Muhammed was going to be a major blow to Abu. Now Dolo was going to set up a plan to relieve Abu of some of his money.

Chapter 15

Dolo knew for him to pull his plan off successfully, he was going to need some help, and he was going to try and get it from an unlikely source.

After the robbery at Shannon's, Dolo had started gathering intel on TNT and Face. TNT was run by a brother and sister by the name of Ogun and Oshun. Both were originally from Africa, and they came with a ruthlessness that was rarely, if ever, seen from teenagers. Oshun was the oldest, but also the smallest. Oshun was a dwarf; at nineteen, she only stood about 4'0" and weighed around a hundred and thirty pounds. She was thick as fuck! Oshun had a grown woman body. Both of the siblings were dark-chocolate with high cheekbones, full lips and deep-set eyes. What most people didn't realize about TNT was that it was two cliques in one. TNT stood for Turbans and Tiaras. Turban Gang was the clique that consisted of mainly dudes, run by Ogun, who was sixteen. They always chanted: *Turban Gang*. They were easily identified because wearing turbans was their signature. Tiara Gang was run by Oshun and it was made up of girls only. The girls under Oshun were more ruthless than the dudes; they didn't have any picks. And it didn't matter who you were, what set you claimed, or who you prayed to.

Face was a different breed altogether! Face, which was short for Scarface, had the nightlife on lock in the state. Any strip club or club in the state that was worth anything was run and owned by Face. He got the name *Scarface* because he had a scar under his right eye and he loved the movie titled *Scarface*. He also ran the most lethal group of jackboys on the East coast known as Jack Boy Mafia or JBM. Face had taken all the notorious robbers from around his way and convinced them to all play for the same team. Face's wifey had started the all-girl team of robbers called Jack Girl Mafia or JGM. Face was a 6'2", brown-skinned dude with an athletic build. Every source that Dolo conferred with about Face said that he was just plain ol' stupid. But not stupid in the aspect of being a dummy; he was stupid in the aspect of: he didn't give a fuck about nothing! But he was a thinker too. They said he used to be wilder but the death of his pregnant wife had slowed him all the way down over the years. The only good thing about it was that they were able to save the baby.

And that was why Dolo was meeting with Ogun and Oshun instead of Face.

"What exactly are you wanting us to do?" Ogun questioned Dolo.

Dolo had reached out and told the two that he wanted to meet them, and allowed them to choose the spot, which put Dolo at a disadvantage because they had told him to meet them at Kickback Jacks, a place Dolo felt like they had an ownership stake in. No matter what day it was, TNT was always deep inside; at the moment, there were probably fifty TNT members milling about.

"I want you to do what you do best—*terrorize*! And you're going to get paid to do it," Dolo said, taking the two in.

Ogun folded his arms across his chest, making his chest poke out in the gray Prada sweater he was wearing. At sixteen, Ogun was already 6'0" and weighed two hundred pounds. He wore his silky black hair in two Fishbones. He had on about a-quarter-million-dollars' worth jewelry. He had on a big face bust down. The Presidential Rolex that was shining under the light. But the piece that caught your attention was the TNT chain. It was an inch-thick Cuban link with the TNT medallion that was all black and green diamonds.

"Once again what are you wanting us to do?" Ogun started to get impatient.

Dolo looked at Oshun, who had not spoken a word since they sat down. She was just sitting there looking around like she had better stuff to do. Dolo was losing his patience because he knew in actuality he could do the shit himself.

"I want you to blow some shit up, plain and simple."

"What are you willing to pay?" Ogun asked.

"A hundred thousand."

"Not enough," he said flatly. Oshun still hadn't uttered a word.

"Two hundred—nothing more, nothing less," Dolo said.

"Still not enough," Ogun smirked.

"Yea, okay." Dolo stood to go.

"Nigga, don't nobody give a fuck about you being in your feelings! You better look around you and realize where you are at!" Ogun bossed up.

Dolo smirked and said, "Obviously you do care and you might want to realize that I don't give a fuck about where I'm at, lil' boy." Dolo was ready to bust Ogun's arrogant-ass dome.

"Tali! Tali!" Ogun shouted and stood up.

Before Dolo knew it, they were surrounded by TNT members.

"What the fuck are y'all waiting on? Please do something so I can show y'all how a real killer gives it up," Dolo growled.

Ogun started moving in Dolo's direction.

"Ogun—no," Oshun spoke softly, but Ogun stopped in his tracks.

Oshun stood up and walked up, and it was at that point Dolo saw that she was a head turner! Oshun was wearing some pink leggings that were so tight you could see the hairs on her pussy through them. Then, the tight white top she had on showcased her flat stomach and D-cups. She flipped her shoulder-length faux locs out of her face as she approached Dolo.

"Are you suicidal or something?" Oshun asked in her low, soft voice, making Dolo strain to hear her over the noise.

"Suicidal—no. Or perhaps yea. Put yourself in my shoes, would you not carry the same way? My gun goes off just like everybody else. I lied, my gun goes off more and with more lethalness!" Dolo bragged.

"What's all the gun talk?" someone asked from behind Dolo.

"Dolo turned and locked eyes with Face, whose voice he'd heard behind him. Face had a look of total relaxation, which puzzled Dolo because, if he really wanted to, he could kill Face in his seat. Seating next to him was a chocolate beauty called Diqueena. Face must've felt the energy behind Dolo's words.

"That's to say I'm all the way with the bullshit!" Dolo matched Face's stare.

"But you ain't with the level of bullshit that I'm gonna come with," Ogun spoke up.

"Chill, goonie. Dolo here is good money, plus I know for a fact that y'all are cut from the same cloth," Face said.

"That two hundred is a go," Oshun looked up at Dolo, letting him know that she had the final say.

Dolo and Oshun held eye contact as he made his exit. Dolo had to focus now because it was about to get real bloody.

Chapter 16

Muhammed's laptop proved to be more valuable than Dolo and Sade originally thought. There was information about the terrorist attack that Abu was funding. The plan of the terrorists was to kill the President of the United States. They were going to do a mass shooting at Duke University and bide their time. They knew sooner or later the president was going to do a speech at the school. Then their plan was to detonate a bomb underground that was going to blow the gas line up that ran under the university, killing everyone on campus. Then Sade had seen on Abu's schedule that he would be coming to the States in the next few months.

Dolo had given Oshun the addresses to all the Arab stores that Abu owned in the States, and gave her specific instructions on what to do. Under no circumstances were the Arab stores to be left standing. The only thing Dolo wanted was an empty lot. Dolo was going to take care of the BP's himself, since they generated more revenue than the Arab stores. He didn't want any mishaps when it came to the BP's. Dolo was about to cost Abu some major figures. If everything went how it was supposed to go, then Dolo estimated he was about to cost Abu a billion dollars. Dolo was going to let TNT do their damage first, then he was going to do his part.

"You trying to ride with me?" Dolo asked Sade.

"Where are you about to go?" she asked.

"I need to swing by Jigga's for a minute."

"Let me go grab my purse real quick."

While he waited, Dolo went and started the Denali he'd gotten Candy to rent. Melissa had Chadijah, so they didn't have to worry about her. Every chance she got, Melissa would come and get Chadijah. Shannon said her daughter had baby fever. Melissa was starting to want kids of her own, and her biological clock was starting to tick.

"I wish you would've changed," Dolo told Sade when she hopped in the truck.

Sade was sporting a pair of blue jeans that, in Dolo's opinion, were two sizes too small. They were so tight you could see her lips through the jeans.

"I'm grown," she brushed him off.

"Whatever!" Dolo pulled off.

Before they got to Jigga's, Dolo stopped at McDonalds and got a fifty-piece nugget and a large iced tea for himself, a Number Two with four sodas, and a Big Mack with no Mac sauce. Anytime Dolo met with Jigga, he would usually get him his favorite meal because Dolo could remember times when he was a jit: Jigga would bring him something to eat. Jigga stayed in a mansion off Ramsey Street out by Pine Forest High School. There was no denying the fact that Jigga's property was top-notch. Jigga had a circular white brick driveway with a marble statue in the middle of it of himself, holding stacks of money and a stick on his waist. Dolo parked behind Jigga's blood-red Ferrari and they got out. Jigga's maid answered the door and let them in.

"Jigga's in the game room," she said and led them to where Jigga was.

Damn! Jigga's mansion is dope, Dolo thought to himself as he feasted his eyes on everything while he walked through. What he liked most about it wasn't the infinity edge swimming pool, or the movie theater, but the high-vaulted ceilings. On the ceiling was a painted scene of the devil in hell with all his demons around him. It was some shit Dolo had never seen before. When they walked into the room,

Jigga was sitting the front of his sixty-inch flat-screen TV, watching the Buffalo Bills beat the hell out of the Pittsburgh Steelers. Jigga had a real game room. He had everything from pinball machines and air hockey to *Ms. Pac-Man*, *Street Fighter*, and *Mortal Kombat*, along with a pool table that sat in the center of the room.

"Here they are, Jigga," the maid said and walked out. Dolo watched the sway of her thick hips under the dress she was wearing. She was Hispanic-looking with a perfectly made body. She was about forty, but she looked way younger. She looked back over her shoulder and caught Dolo looking.

"Damn, nigga, you thirsty as hell!" Jigga laughed, watching Dolo watching the maid. That act can have yo ass paying all her bills. What it do, Sade?"

"I'm chilling," Sade responded.

"What brings y'all to my humble abode?"

"I need you to talk to your people for me—I need some more of that C-4," Dolo told him.

"Damn, nigga, you ain't playing no games."

"I can't because Abu ain't playing no games with me. I'm trying to take the nigga all the way down through there. When I get through with him, he will curse the day he decided to put some money on my head," Dolo said confidently.

"Dolo, I'm with you a hundred and ten percent but you need to go ahead and cripple him. You don't poke a sleeping bear unless you have a real big gun. True, he put a bag on your head but he ain't really pushed the issue because it's only been two attempts on your life. Dolo, if he really starts to get nasty, you'll be ducking bullets every time you open your eyes. And I'm sure Sade can attest to that!" Jigga said and Sade nodded.

"Truthfully, I don't give a fuck about it. When he shows himself, I'ma bust his brains, no questions asked, and I can almost guarantee that eventually he's gonna show his face and when he do—"

"I'm with you, my nigga. How many of them thangs do you need?"

"Twenty."

"I gotta make a call and I should have them within the next four hours," said Jigga.

"Hey, girl!" Melissa said, walking into the game room with Chadijah in her arms, looking sexy. Melissa had on some red skinny jeans that had her butt sitting up just right, a tight red long-sleeved shirt with no bra. So, her nipples were poking out. She wore some white red bottom stilettos, and her shoulder-length hair was blown out.

"Hey, Lissa. Hey, boo boo!" Sade kissed Chadijah, who immediately laid her head on Dolo's chest and closed her eyes.

"Where is my hug at, boy?" Melissa stepped to Dolo, smiling.

"What have you been up to?" He gave her a half hug.

"Same ol' same ol'. You know me, but I got something I need to talk to you about," Melissa said seriously.

Dolo walked to the other side of the room and asked, "What's good?"

"I want to get back in and I know you need me. Who else is gonna watch your back like you know I can? Nigga, you know we're the same breed times ten. Shit! I'm being all the way honest, I'm more with the shits than you are," she whispered.

Dolo bit back his retort because when he really thought about it, it wasn't that she was more with the shit than him; it was that her level of hate was higher than his.

"Plus when shit starts to heat up and Al-Qaeda get to trying to blow your shit up, you know I can match that energy," Melissa continued.

"Okay, girl, you're in but we're going about this differently. I'll give you the rundown later," he relented.

"It's impolite to whisper," Sade intoned.

"Oh girl, hush. I needed to holler at your brother about something real quick," said Melissa as they rejoined Sade and Jigga.

"Bra, I'll have those in two hours," Jigga told Dolo.

"A'ight. I'll be back through here. I'ma call you later, Melissa." Dolo walked out.

"What did Melissa want?" Sade inquired when they got in the truck.

"She was ready to blow some smoke." Dolo pulled out onto Ramsey Street.

"Stop at the CVS right quick. I need to get me some tampons," Sade said.

Dolo pulled into the CVS and Sade went inside. While he was waiting, he turned around and started playing peek-a-boo with Chadijah. It started pouring down; before Sade came back, the rain clouds had the sky dark like it was midnight.

"Where?" Sade hopped back in the truck. Dolo pulled out and got back on Ramsey, heading downtown. As they neared the social services building, Melissa pulled up beside them in the blue Mustang GT with the black racing stripe down the side and honked her horn. Dolo blew his horn and swerved in front of her.

"Boy, the road slick to be playing them kinda games, especially with my baby back there!" Sade chastised him. Dolo peeked at Chadijah in the rearview mirror and saw her smiling.

"She's okay."

Dolo drove downtown and was making his way around the market house when a F-250 pulled up alongside him and rolled their window down.

"Get down!" Dolo yelled and jerked the wheel as his window shattered.

Boc! Boc! Boc! The shooter was airing the truck out. Dolo was more worried about getting his niece to safety than shooting back. Sade then reached in the back and grabbed the Mac 90 off the floor and started shooting at the pick-up.

Kah! Kah! Kah! Sade was sending rounds in front of Dolo's face into the F-250.

"Hold on!" Dolo jerked the wheel to the left and hit the F-250.

It was then that Dolo noticed that it was the same woman who had tried to kill them the other time by pulling them over as if she was a cop.

Boom! Boom! Boom! Melissa pulled up and started shooting a cannon at the F-250, causing it to go off the road and crash into the Airborne Museum sign.

"Go kill that bitch!" Sade yelled to Melissa. Dolo kept driving because he didn't want to be anywhere near the scene when the police came. Then, the truck shut off. Dolo tried to start the truck up so the engine wouldn't turn over.

"Fuck!" Dolo yelled, and it was then that Chadijah started crying. "Come on, we gotta get out of here."

"Freeze! Don't move!"

Dolo turned to see two cops with their guns in his face; they put him and Sade in separate cars. All he could hope was that this time they were real police.

Chapter 17

"Mr. Mallory, do you know that we can charge you with first-degree kidnapping, weapon possession and witness tampering? That's not to mention the killing of an FBI agent. Which will get you the death penalty!" the white detective said.

After putting Dolo in the police cruiser, they took him to the police station and stuck him in a bland room that Dolo knew was the interrogation room. He'd been sitting there for the last three hours. He hadn't seen any sign of Sade or his niece.

"If you could charge me with any of any of those charges, you would've done it already." Dolo was a hundred percent sure they didn't have anything on him.

"Oh, he's a bad ass, Mike. We'll see how bad he is when he's sitting on death row," the white detective said to his partner.

His partner was a tall, slim black dude with a fade. He was acting as if he was on Dolo's side.

"Let's go ahead and cut through this bullshit, okay? Let me call my lawyer." Dolo said the words that all cops hated to hear.

The minute he said the word lawyer, they got up and walked out, leaving him by himself. Dolo leaned back in the hard steel chair and put his hands behind his head. He didn't have a care in the world. All he had to do was wait until they came and released him. Dolo looked around the room again.

There wasn't anything in the room except three chairs divided by a wooden table, a one-way tinted mirror and a camera. The walls were painted a dull grey. Someone had written: *Fuck 12* all over the table. The door to the room had a small square window that Dolo hadn't seen a soul go by.

Dolo had a nagging thought that kept popping up into his head. Who the hell was this bitch that kept trying to kill them? He knew it was coming from the bounty that was on his head. But Dolo didn't know how she kept finding him. If she could find him, it was possible for other killers to find him. *Boom! Boom!* Two big explosion rocked the building so hard the wall cracked. *Kah! Kah! Kat! Pop! Pop! Pop! Tat! Tat! Tat! Boc! Boc!* Dolo heard all kinds of guns being fired. It sounded like a gun range. He rushed to the door to look out and saw police running up and down the hallway. Then, the building's lights went out. *Fuck that!* Dolo thought. He pushed the table up against the wall so he would have some room. He took a few steps back, lunged forward with his right leg, and kicked the door halfway off the hinges. The emergency lights had clicked on, casting shadows across the walls. The inside of the building sounded like an Afghanistan battlefield. He crept out of the room and went looking for Sade. Dolo started checking the other rooms in the hallway. He went into the room that was on the other side of the one-way mirror and found a Sig Sauer .10mm. He cocked it and stepped out. He checked every room on the hallways. It wasn't until he got to the last room on the hall that he found Sade holding a sleeping Chadijah.

"Oh my God! Are you alright?" Sade asked Dolo.

"Yes, we need to get out of here!" Dolo led her out of the room.

"Allahu Akbar!" An Arab bent the corner, wielding a choppa. Dolo put two slugs from the Sig into his face.

"That's a bad sign," Sade said.

"What makes you say that?" Dolo asked while peeking around the corner.

"Because he was an Al-Qaeda suicide bomber. Look at the vest he's wearing," she pointed out. Abu must've gotten the message that he wasn't dealing with a peon, so now he was sending the big boys, and they were coming hard too. To attack the police station in downtown Fayetteville, trying to kill them, spelled urgency and desperation. Dolo handed Sade the Sig, and he grabbed the AK-47 off of the suicide bomber. He needed to get them out of there asap.

Boom! Another explosion rocked the building, the fire alarm went off, and the sprinklers cut on. Dolo led Sade down the alley into another one. There was smoke all through the building, making it hard to see. A group of Al-Qaeda soldiers was up ahead with their back towards them. Dolo pulled Sade and Chadijah into a room. He looked around and saw that they were in a room with a bunch of police uniforms.

That's it. An idea came to Dolo.

He started searching for a uniform in his size. He found one, stripped down and put it on. He'd found a vest and handed it to Sade. He held Chadijah while Sade put the vest on. The entire time, Chadijah had been quiet; she was just looking around. Dolo grabbed a helmet and donned it. Dolo handed Chadijah back to Sade, peeked out the door, and saw the group of Al-Qaeda soldiers still standing there. He sent a burst from the choppa into their backs, sending them to the floor in pain.

"Come on! Come on!" Dolo urged.

They made it to the steps, and as they were descending the steps, an Arab was coming up.

"Allahu Akbar!" he screamed and reached for the cord on his chest.

Kah! Kah! Dolo shot him in the throat, killing him before he could pull the cord.

Dolo kicked him over, took the vest off of him and slung it over his shoulder.

And what are you going to do with that?" questioned Sade.

"You'll see."

Dolo didn't know how he was going to get them out of the building because when they got to the first floor, the Al-Qaeda were shooting it out with the police. The stairwell was in a position that, if they walked out, it was a real good chance they would get seen

"Allahu Akbar!"

Booooom! An Al-Qaeda soldier ran out the front towards the police and pulled the cord on his suicide vest. Dolo used the explosion as a distraction. He pulled Sade out and they made their way to the back of the building.

"Sade, give me the baby." An Arab stepped out of the shadows in a police uniform.

"Sayyid, y'all are not taking my baby. You're going to have to kill me first."

"Okay." He lifted the pistol in his hands, but Dolo was already squeezing the trigger on the AK-47.

The bullets sent Sayyid reeling backwards. Dolo yanked Sade down the hallway and around another corner where another group of Al-Qaeda were standing by the backdoor. Dolo hurriedly threw the suicide vest towards the group. It landed about three feet from the group. Dolo pushed Sade back behind the corner and started shooting at the vest. *Boom!* The vest exploded, blowing the Al-Qaeda soldiers up and knocking the back wall down. Dolo flipped the visor of the helmet down and pulled Sade out of the hole in the wall. It looked like the whole police force was out there.

"Move! Move! I have to get them to safety!" Dolo said from behind the helmet.

SWAT team members rushed up to them and led them to safety. Once they got them to the perimeter, the SWAT team dashed back off because the Al-Qaeda started shooting out of their windows. Dolo led Sade to a police cruiser, and they got in. It was then that Chadijah started to wail at the top of her young lungs. Dolo crunk the car up and pulled out without anyone noticing.

"Who was that dude in the police uniform?" Dolo asked as he speed-balled away from the police station.

"That was Sayyid. He's Abu's first cousin and a lieutenant in Al-Qaeda. Dolo, I'm terrified of him. I've seen him in videos doing some heinous things to women and kids."

"You're safe, I got you. What did the detectives say to you during your interrogation?"

"They asked whether you had kidnapped me and all types of other questions, but I cleared your name. I told them that you were my brother and that you were protecting me." She bounced Chadijah, trying to get her to calm down.

"What does Allahu Akbar mean?"

"Allah is the greatest."

They rode the rest of the way in silence. They had survived a major attempt on their life. Now it was Dolo's turn to make a move. When he got done, Abu was going to be saying: *Dolo is the greatest*.

Chapter 18

Dolo and Sade woke up the next morning on their bullshit! Melissa told them that when she pulled up to the F-250, the driver had already gotten missing. So, wherever the chick was, Dolo knew they were going to be seeing her again, only now he was going to be ready when she popped up. Dolo was going to be expecting her to pop out, and when she did, he was going to send her to the gates of hell. Sade uploaded the video of Muhammed getting eaten by the alligators to the Al-Qaeda channel that they aired the beheadings of people they captured on; she was hundred percent sure that Abu was going to see it. This move was more mental than physical. You could beat someone mentally and never have to lay a hand on them. And that was the game that Dolo was playing with Abu. It was the beginning of the chess game, and Dolo was bringing his bishops and knights out to attack.

***

"Yea, that's right. I want all of them to be hit at the same time," Dolo told Oshun.

"You are asking for a whole lot. It was tough enough coordinating all this shit. Now you're trying to get a lil' extra."

"You ain't paying us enough for all of that," Ogun added.

"Look, there's a reason I'm telling you to do it like this. I really need it done like that, Oshun. Make this happen for me," Dolo said, staring at Oshun, totally ignoring Ogun.

"Okay," Oshun nodded.

Oshun was sweet on Dolo; Ogun could see it, and he wasn't really feeling it.

"You want a drink?" a bartender asked Dolo. They were at the Sky Bar, a bar downtown that catered to the who's who. It was common to see the mayor, high-end lawyers and judges. It was nothing to see J. Cole there having drinks. The bar was called the Sky Bar because the roof of the bar was glass, and you could look up into the sky. During the day, there was a shade that they could pull over it to give the patrons a break from the sun. There were floor-to-ceiling windows all around the bar, so that you could see downtown in any direction. The circular shaped bar sat in the middle of the floor. There were twenty seats around the bar. The floor of the bar had white neon lights scattered through it. There were twenty tables with black sofas all around the floor. Then, on two walls, there were booths you could sit in, giving you a better view. The bartenders were all women, and every one of them looked like they could grace the cover of a magazine.

"No, he's good—he got one," Oshun said sharply. Dolo chuckled. He was going to use the crush that she had on him to his advantage. The bartender gave him a look, then sashayed away. Dolo downed his orange juice and said: "So what am I gonna drink now?"

"What are you drinking?" Oshun asked.

"Orange juice."

Oshun walked away towards the bar. Jigga watched her ass jiggle in the black leggings she had on.

"I don't know what you got going on, but I need you to know this. And make sure you listen closely. That's my heart right there. I'll lay my life down for her. I see she's crushing on you. She's grown and she is older than me, so she can make her own decision but let's be clear. If you hurt her in any way, I'mma rip your heart out and eat that shit!" Ogun threatened

"Lil' boy, it's absolutely nothing you can do with me, believe that. We're not the same breed. You may be a killer and all that, but I'm more devilish than the Devil himself."

"Hmm." Ogun cast a menacing glance at Dolo. Dolo returned the look with fire in his own eyes. Just then, Oshun returned. "I'm 'bout to go line shit up," Ogun said to Oshun. "Are you going to be good?" he asked, pulling his orange Moncler coat on.

"As long as she is with me she is good," Dolo said assuredly, causing Oshun to start blushing. Ogun hugged Oshun and left, leaving the two alone.

"Were you leaving with me?" Dolo asked and she shrugged shyly.

"Let's go." Dolo stood and waited for Oshun to grab her things.

"Where are we going?" she questioned, still sitting at the table.

"Wherever you want to."

"The beach," she said.

"I don't know about all that but I'm ready to get out of here. Are you coming with me or nah?" Oshun looked at him, contemplating whether or not she wanted to leave with Dolo.

"Okay," she got up and pulled her hoody on. They got outside and Dolo helped her up into the Suburban. Dolo palmed her ass as he held here up. Her ass was so soft that Dolo knew if he ever got behind her, her ass was going to be moving like it had a mind of its own.

"Don't touch my ass anymore," Osun said. Dolo did not respond, he just grinned.

"How did you get into business of killing people?" she asked.

Dolo weighed the questions. "If I'm being honest, it was just something I enjoyed and I was good at it. Very good. It's something about seeing the life fade out of someone's eyes that gives me a rush. Once I found out that I could get paid for killing, it was a wrap. I didn't look back since."

"I thought my little brother was the craziest person I knew, but now that I've met you, you've earned that spot," she said with an easy smirk.

"What does that say about you then being that you're in a truck by yourself with the craziest person you know?" he raised a brow.

"It says that I'm not worried because if push came to shove I'd kill you before you had the chance to do anything crazy to me!" Oshun vowed with a look in her eyes that said she was dead serious. "And where are you going?" she questioned, seeing that they are on I-95.

"Sit your sexy ass back and ride. You're in good hands." He put his hand on her thigh.

"Boy, boo!" Oshun swatted his hand away. Dolo cut on Young Bleu's album, pushed the speedometer to eighty, and cut the cruise control on. Oshun reclaimed her seat, closed her eyes and listened to Young Bleu sing about a girl being his. Candy sent Dolo a text asking him if they were going to chill tonight. He texted her back saying tomorrow and she sent him the devil emoji. Dolo was gonna fuck around and cut Candy the fuck off. She kept trying to act like they were exclusive, and they weren't.

"What am I doing?" Oshun whispered, as though she was having second thoughts.

"What you say?" Dolo asked.

"Let me out."

"Say what?" Dolo was confused.

"Let me the fuck out or I'll kill you right now!" Oshun said, barely above a whisper, and produced a wicked-looking knife and put it to Dolo's neck. The look she had was one of utter seriousness. Dolo pulled over. Oshun leapt out of the truck and disappeared into the wood line off of the highway. Dolo pulled off; he wasn't about to deal with no crazy-ass young bitch!

Chapter 19

"Dolo!" Sade yelled from downstairs.

"What the fuck are you yelling about, woman?" Dolo came down the stairs.

"Look! Look!" She pointed at the flat-screen TV mounted on the living room wall.

Dolo looked and saw the viral news on the TV.

"Cut it up right quick," he said.

"A string of attacks on Middle Eastern-owned gas stations has the U.S. on high alert," the news anchor stated. "Twenty-five gas stations have been attacked and blown up simultaneously with unknown explosives. The FBI and ATF have taken over the investigation. They are treating the recent bombings as acts of terrorism. All twenty-five gas stations have been completely levelled."

"Eat!" Dolo yelled and called Melissa.

"Do you know what time it is?" Melissa cracked, obviously having just woke up.

"Yea, I do. This the time to get active. I'll be there in about thirty minutes and if you're not ready, I'm leaving"

"Urrghh!" she screamed and Dolo hung up.

TNT had done their job almost better than Dolo could have. Now it was Dolo's turn and he had to outshine TNT. He went upstairs and put on all-black from head to toe. Dolo went to his weapons room and grabbed a Beretta 92F .9mm.

"Where are you about to go?" Sade asked, standing off to the side.

"To cost Abu a lot of money"

"I'm coming too. I don't wanna just sit around and do nothing."

"Not this time. I got Melissa coming. You ain't never been in a hostile situation before. Your thought process in the field has to be razor-sharp. A slow reaction could mean one or both of our lives." Dolo schooled her. Sade nodded like she understood. Dolo grabbed the duffel bag full of C-4 and walked to the front of the house. The alarm at the gate chimed, letting him know that there was someone at the gate. Dolo went and looked at his security feed and saw Candy's car outside of the gate. He shook his head. He'd told her last time that she needed to call before popping up. Dolo hit the button to open the gate. He went to the front door and stepped out.

"Hey, baby!" Candy greeted Dolo.

"What's up? Why do you keep doing shit that I tell you not to?" asked Dolo.

"Are you really gonna trip on me right now? I came over here to give you some of this good pussy and you are acting like a bitch." Candy snapped.

"Make that your last time calling my brother a bitch!" Sade stepped into the doorway.

"Lil' girl, you just got in the picture! I been here! So stay outta our business and find you some of your own to attend to!" Candy dismissed her.

"I'm so sick of that thot," Sade said to Dolo.

"It takes one to know one, hoe." Candy glared.

"Y'all get off the dumb shit! Matter of fact, go in the house, Sade. Candy, I'll get with you when I get back."

"You ain't going nowhere but with me," Candy mushed Dolo in the head.

"Oh, you got shit fucked up!" Sade tried to walk towards Candy but Dolo stepped in her way.

"Sade, be an adult, I got her."

"Yea, bitch, he got me!" Candy said, shaking her neck as Sade shook her head going back in the house.

"I'm done with you, Candy. You too fucking extra." Dolo tried to step around her but she got in his way.

"Baby, please!" she begged.

Dolo was about to go around him when a green dot appeared on Candy's forehead. Dolo spun around just as Sade was pulling the trigger on the Glock slim line 36. The bullet slapped Candy dead in the center of the forehead, blowing the back of her head out. Dolo looked back and Sade was casually walking back in the house. He looked at Candy sprawled out in his driveway with a puddle of blood forming under her, and shook his head. He picked her body up and carried her to the gator pen. The gators were all at the water's edge with their mouths open. Dolo dropped Candy's body two feet from the water and walked out. That was a waste of some good pussy. When Dolo got back to the front of the house, Melissa was driving up the driveway in her Mustang.

"You said thirty minutes," Melissa said, rolling the windows down.

"Man, Sade killed Candy and I had to get rid of the body. Now I gotta dump her car." Dolo grabbed the duffle off the steps and put it in Melissa's car.

"Are you serious?" she laughed. "That's that Mallory blood running through her veins."

"Follow me." Dolo got in Candy's car and drove off. Dolo parked the car in the Wal-Mart parking lot and got in with Melissa.

"Where to now?"

"Wilmington. We need to go the port and we need to hurry up and get there before one o'clock." Dolo started pulling the C-4 out of the duffle bag, making sure the adhesive on the back was in working order.

"What is that stuff?" Melissa inquired, pushing the V-8 to a hundred.

"It's C-4. Basically, it's a bomb. I'm going to stick all of these to the BP tankers and blow them all up at one time. Every BP that Abu owns on the east coast is going to have a shortage of gas." Dolo carefully placed them all back in the duffel.

Dolo leaned his seat back and closed his eyes. After this move right here, Abu was going to have to come to the U.S. and clear things up with his companies. Dolo was going to make it his last trip abroad. Dolo dozed off and didn't wake back up until they were pulling into Wilmington.

"Drive to the port and park."

"What do you need me to do?" she questioned.

"Watch my back and if shit turns sour, bust your gun." Dolo got out.

Dolo passed an unmanned security booth where he snagged a jacket that said: *Port Security*. Dolo knew that there were four tankers full of gas, all of which were Abu's. They were to be docked at KS-212, KS-214 and KS-215.The laptop said that each one was going to be carrying 50 million gallons of gas. Dolo walked along the park until he saw KS-212.

"Damn," Dolo whistled. The tankers were humongous. Each one was about as long as a football field. He walked across the boardwalk near the tanker and was immediately stopped by a burly white guy.

"Who are you?"

"I'm port security and I'm here to take a look at your cargo," Dolo shot a lie out.

"They already do that," the guy spat a chunk of chewing tobacco by Dolo's foot.

Dolo's hands shot out, striking him in the throat, crushing his windpipe. Then, he pushed the dude off the side of the boat. Dolo was moving before his body hit the water. He walked along the ship and struck five bundles of C-4 in different locations. Dolo did the same thing to the other three without incident and made his way back to Melissa's car.

"What happened? Why didn't I see anything blow up?"

"Damn, you wanted me to blow up with them?" Dolo pulled out a cylinder tube. "Drive away. The explosion is going to be massive. That was enough C-4 to level two city blocks. So, combine that with all that gas, and you have a major bomb."

When they were a mile away, Dolo hit the detonator and blew the C-4. The explosions were so loud and powerful they felt the ground shake. The fire from the explosions shot up like mushroom clouds from an atomic bomb. Dolo knew without a shadow of a doubt that a ten hundred-million-gallon loss of oil was a nice chunk of money, considering the fact that gas was almost four dollars a gallon. And Dolo wasn't done; every time a shipment of Abu's gas came in, he was going to blow them up. Dolo's bishop had just taken one of Abu's knights; now it was Abu's turn to move.

Chapter 20

The next morning, Dolo was lying in the bed watching the news, listening to them talk about the BP tankers blowing up. Not only had the BP tankers blown up, but every ship within three hundred yards was sunk, and the dock had been utterly destroyed.

"Sean!" Sade walked into his bedroom looking like she'd seen a ghost.

"What's up?" Dolo asked and she handed him her phone.

"Yo," Dolo grabbed the phone.

"You've became a thorn in my side—you're like a gnat that won't go away," a man with a heavy Middle Eastern accent said.

Immediately, Dolo knew who it was. Abu!

"You're going to earn yourself an extremely slow death."

"Like Muhammed did? Abu, if you plan on living a long and prospering life and living long enough to spend all of the money you have, you'll rescind the bounty you have on our heads. If not, I'm going to see to it that you die with a pork chop in your mouth."

"Dolo, you seem to have a false sense of security. I can crush you at will. You are still breathing because I allow it. Consider yourself dead!" Abu said confidently.

"Do you what you have to do but don't get caught lacking because if I catch you with your pants down you're a dead man." Dolo hit the end button.

"I don't know why you're looking so shocked! That motherfucka ain't talking about a bitch ass thang! I'ma slump that fool the first chance I get!" Dolo stated with passion.

"Okay. Are we going to see grandma today?" Sade changed the subject.

"Yea, but I got to run a few errands first." Dolo got up.

"I'm going with you."

"Not with that thing you got on." Sade was wearing a pair of leggings that was so tight you could count the hairs on her pussy.

Sade stormed out of his room puffing and hurting. Dolo went to the bathroom, washed his face, brushed his teeth, and looked into his closet to find something to wear.

"What do you think I should wear, Sasha?" he asked her as she walked into the closet behind him. Sasha cocked her head to the side.

"You ain't no help."

Dolo grabbed a blue and gray thermal, a blue and gray toboggan, and some blue and gray Air Max 95's. He put on a lightweight vest under his thermal. Dolo put on his blue G-Shock and rose-gold rosary. He walked downstairs to the kitchen and warmed up three slices of the leftover pizza that Sade had ordered last night.

"Your ass better be ready by the time I get done eating this pizza!" he yelled.

"I been ready." Sade walked into the room wearing a green and white Nike sweat suit, carrying Chadijah.

"Go in there and put on one of those vests." Dolo grabbed his niece.

Chadijah immediately reached for the slice of pizza that Dolo had in his other hand. He sat her in her high chair, tore a little piece of the pizza and put it in her mouth. She started bouncing up and down the minute Dolo put it in her mouth.

"Boy, I know you ain't feeding my baby no pizza!" Sade yelled, coming back into the room.

"She got a few teeth. She good."

Sade grabbed Chadijah out of the chair and walked out to the rental car. Dolo followed behind her and climbed in.

"Where are we going?"

"I need to holla at Jigga about some shit." Jigga's restaurant—Soul City—was super crowded. Sade grabbed a seat while Dolo went to the back to talk to Jigga. Dolo walked into Jigga's office and could instantly tell that he was in a bad mood.

"What the hell is wrong witchu?" Dolo sat down across from Jigga.

"Somebody has been robbing my spots lately and they've been coming off! I got hit last night for twenty bricks of heroin. In the last three weeks I've lost thirty million dollars in dope."

"So you have any idea who it is?"

"Nah because they kill everybody in the spot when they hit it so I don't have anybody to question," Jigga said in frustration. "And you've been busy too. I don't think Abu was ready for that move. You had to have set him back a grip financially."

"I talked to him, he called Sade. He was talking crazy as hell. He said he hasn't given me his undivided attention and that he could crush me at will and some other bullshit!" Dolo said in disbelief.

"Dolo, *do not* play with him, kill him when you get the chance. Stay on point because blowing up all that gas definitely has Abu's attention. He's going to be gunning for you now and—truth be told—I don't think you can go toe to toe with him."

"Only because of all the resources he has at his disposal but that's where guerilla tactics come into play. I'm sticking and moving. The reason I'm here is because I need a knight's armament SR-23 MK II sniper rifle. And I need exploding rounds to go with it."

"I'm not even going to ask you what you need it for. I'll have it in a few days."

"Next time I come though I'll have you a Big Mac with no mac sauce." Dolo laughed and walked out.

"Are we going to see granny now?" asked Sade.

"Yea."

Dolo drove to Heavenly Comforts, where their grandmother was. They walked to the sign-in desk and got their visitor passes. Dolo and Sade walked to the room, and she wasn't there. There weren't too many places she could've been. They walked around looking for her. Then, it came to Dolo where she probably was. He knew she loved to walk around outside. She particularly loved the rose garden.

"You got me doing a lot of walking—she's getting heavy," Sade complained.

"Let me see her." Dolo was getting ready to grab Chadijah when he saw his grandma sitting on a bench in the rose garden talking to another woman with their backs to them.

"There go granny. I want you to start walking. Your butt is getting heavy," Dolo told Chadijah. Dolo watched as Sade got to his grandma and the other lady. When Sade got to his grandmother, the other woman stood up pointing a pistol at Sade. Dolo pulled his gun and was about to shoot but his grandma stood up in his way, blocking his view.

Boc! Boc! She shot Sade twice in the chest and she crumpled to the ground. Dolo's grandma grabbed the woman's hand. It was then that Dolo got a good look at the other woman and recognized her as the woman who'd been trying to kill them. They locked eyes and her eyes got this hateful look. His grandma followed the woman's eyes and Dolo.

"Sean!" Her eyes got big.

Dolo was stuck! He was holding Chadijah with one arm in the way of him killing a woman that was dead set on trying to kill him.

"Move, Nah-Nah!" Dolo yelled.

"No!" she said and looked at the woman. "Sammy, it's time to let him know.

By this time Dolo was close enough to see Sade. Her chest was moving up and down and he didn't see any blood. The vest had saved her. Dolo was able to get an angle where he had a clear line of vision and took the shot.

Instead of hitting her in the dome, the two slugs caught her in the upper chest, throwing her to the ground. Dolo stepped over and pointed the barrel at her face, and his grandma grabbed the barrel.

"To kill her is to kill your father's firstborn child."

Chapter 21

"What are you talking about, Nah-Nah?" Dolo questioned with the gun still trained on the woman.

She grabbed a crying Chadijah from Dolo and said, "It's only one way to tell you. I've wanted to tell you for a while now but she wouldn't allow me to, and I respected her wishes. That's your oldest sister. Samantha." Dolo walked over to Sade and helped her up.

"Stupid bitch tried to kill me! I don't give a fuck who she is. I'ma bout to kill her. Give me the gun." Sade kicked her, yelped and grabbed for her foot.

"What?" Dolo questioned.

"That bitch body is hard as hell."

"Sade! Your mouth," Nah-Nah scolded her

Dolo reached down and touched her and felt that she too had a bulletproof vest on. Her eyes popped and she grabbed Dolo by the throat with one hand and his gun hand with her other. Dolo was more surprised by her strength than her grabbing him. Sade tried to kick Samantha and she caught Dolo in the mouth. Samantha tried to come down with a vicious elbow, and Dolo moved his head to the side, causing her to strike the ground. Dolo grabbed Samantha in a bear hug, and she head butted him in the nose, bringing tears to his eyes.

"Y'all stop right now!" Nah-Nah yelled.

Boc! Boc! Boc! Sade shot Samantha three times in back and she fell over. Dolo grabbed the gun from Sade and was getting ready to shoot Samantha when his grandma screamed. "Sean Marvin Mallory! I swear to gawd if you kill her—"

"She's trying to kill us!" Sade yelled.

"Here." She handed Sade Chadijah and kneeled beside Samantha. Dolo knew she was good because she had on a bullet-proof vest, although she was going to be sore as hell. Their grandma helped Samantha sit up. Dolo and Sade stood back while she helped Samantha up onto the bench. If looks could kill, Dolo and Sade would be in body bags, considering the kind of look Samantha gave them.

"What do y'all have going on? Y'all are flesh and blood. You're supposed to stick together and not hurt each other!" Nah-Nah said.

"I don't even know her," Dolo said.

"For the most part, this is my fault. I should've introduced her to you years ago but she was being stubborn. She didn't want to meet you. But y'all are so much alike. Both of you are in the skin business."

"The skin business?" Sade wondered.

"Ya, the skin business. You don't know what they do for a living? They kill people, baby!" she said flatly.

"Nah-Nah! What are you talking about?" Dolo questioned. He knew she had her suspicions, but this was her first time outright saying it.

"Hush, Sean! Sammy, are you okay?" she asked Samantha as she got her bearings.

"I've got get out of here," Samantha cringed as she stood up looking at the gun in Dolo's hand.

"No you're going to sit here and come to an understanding. I'm not going to live forever! I want all of you to reach a common ground right now. I will *not* have my grandchildren live like this." Ms. Geraldine was usually even tempered and never ever raised her voice.

"Calm down, Nah-Nah." Dolo didn't want her Alzheimer's to worsen.

"The only common ground we're gonna have is their cemetery plots." Samantha stood up.

"Sammy, don't get worked up now. Sit down!" Ms. Geraldine said, and Samantha sat back down. "What is your issue with them?

Samantha stared Dolo and Sade down before saying:

"I didn't have an issue with her, she was just another target but now that I know who her mother is, to hell with her too. They're the reason my life went to shits. If my father had never met their junky ass mama, my mom wouldn't have killed herself and my dad wouldn't have overdosed." Her eyes got misty.

"Watch your mouth!" Dolo said. "Nah-Nah, how is she your grandchild if our mom is your daughter?"

"Because your dad is actually my son." Dolo was at a loss for words. His entire life, he had been under the impression that Nah-Nah was his mother's mom but she was his dad's mom. Not that it would've made a difference because was still his grandmother. She was now the only relative that Dolo knew on his father's side of the family. Dolo didn't know too much about this father, nor did he care to. He'd never done a single thing for Dolo his entire life; so, Dolo didn't give a fuck about him. He'd never even met his pops, and neither had Sade; so, there wasn't an ounce of compassion there. Truth of the matter was that, after his mom died, Dolo didn't care for anyone but Nah-Nah.

"I love you, Nah-Nah, but I really ain't feeling her whole little vibe," Dolo admitted.

"And I ain't feeling yours, nigga!" Samantha responded.

"How can you not like us because of our mother? The things she did, we had nothing to do with. Did she make our father have sex with her? No, so that doesn't have a thing to do with us. We have the snake blood running through our veins. We're one, take it or leave it!" Sade spoke her mind.

"Sade's right," their grandmother stated.

"Come on, Nah-Nah, you've been out here in the cold long enough." Dolo grabbed her hand.

"I'm not going in until you tell me that me that y'all are going to be okay and are going to look after each other."

"We got you, granny," Sade said.

"What about you two?" she questioned Dolo and Samantha.

"I'm good," Dolo stated.

"I'm good too," Samantha added.

"Prove it," their grandma said.

Dolo and Samantha looked at each other for a brief second. Then, Dolo walked over to Samantha and gave her a hug.

"I'm still going to kill you," Samantha whispered in his ear.

"I'm glad y'all got that settled because when I'm gone, y'all are going to need to lean on each other," Nah-Nah said.

They walked their grandma to her room, got her settled and were walking down the hall together towards the exit when they heard someone yell: "Allahu Akbar!" They all knew what that meant. Dolo and Samantha both turned, dropping to one knee with pistols aimed in the direction of the yell. They turned to see an Arab run into their grandmother's room. Dolo took off running back down the hallway towards her room when it exploded, knocking him backwards.

"Noo!" Dolo yelled.

Abu had just killed the only mother he'd ever really known.

Chapter 22

The blast from the explosion knocked Dolo back ten feet. Black smoke billowed out of the room. The fire alarm began blaring and the sprinklers came on, drenching the trio. Dolo got up and ran to the doorway of his grandmother's room. The room was engulfed in flames; the heat was so intense that Dolo couldn't get within the insides of the room.

"Come on, Sean!" Sade urged, tugging his arm. The fire was spreading all the way up the hallway. Dolo knew there was no way his grandmother could have survived the blast.

"Sir, you have to get out of here," a firefighter tried ushering Dolo out of the way.

Dolo pushed him and walked away. Dolo wanted to shed some blood. Sade saw a look in his eyes that she'd never seen before. When they got outside, there were firefighters, police and nurses ushering elderly people away from the building. When they got to the rental, Samantha was leaning up against it. Dolo had really forgotten all about her. As they drew closer Dolo could see the tears in her eyes. Dolo wasn't feeling any compassion for her though.

"You got a lot of nerve, bitch! I should blow your top right now." Dolo was in a mood where he just wanted to draw blood, anybody's blood. The only reason he eased up his hammer was because his grandmother's words were playing in the back of his mind. She was supposed to be his older sister, so he was hesitant to snuff her lights out, but that didn't mean that he wouldn't.

"What's the plan now?" Sade asked Samantha. "Are you still going get yourself killed trying to kill us for the man who killed our granny?"

"Let her try! I'm good! I don't need no one to try and get revenge for Nah-Nah, I got that. Ain't nobody here when it was just me and Nah-Nah and I had to do it all. I was the only one providing!" Dolo vented.

"Oh my God!" Sade took a quick intake of breath, looking down at her phone.

"What's up?" Dolo asked.

Sade walked over to Dolo and handed him her phone. Dolo glanced at the screen and his temperature shot to the moon. There was a still shot of his grandmother gagged and bound. It was a bitter-sweet feeling because Dolo knew that his grandma was alive and also that she was in harm's way because of him. The phone rang and Dolo answered it asap.

"Yea."

"Is this Dolo?" Abu's voice came through the ear pieces.

"Your life has officially started its countdown to the end," Dolo promised.

"We're all born to die," Abu stated nonchalantly. "You have something I want and I have something you want. I'll give you your grandmother back for Sade."

"If you so much as touch a hair on her head I'll—"

"Save all the false bravado for someone who believes you," he cut Dolo off mid-sentence. "I don't know who you think you are or who you believe yourself to be but I rub shoulders with killers and bosses. Men who will erase your entire bloodline and not have to lift a finger. Make the BBC news, then I'll be impressed. Now what are you going to do? Save your grandmother or be responsible for her death?" Abu gave Dolo an ultimatum.

Dolo looked at Sade, wondering if he could make the trade and instantly told himself yea. He couldn't choose Sade over Nah-Nah. Sade hadn't been there since day one; she had recently come into his life. Dolo really didn't even know her.

But Nah-Nah had been his rock, his voice of reason since his childhood, so his decision was an easy one.

"Okay, how are we going to do this?" Dolo asked Abu.

"I'll call you in a few days and let you know," he said and ended the call.

"What happened?" Sade asked.

"He wants you for Nah-Nah." Dolo broke the news to her

"When?" asked Samantha.

"He told me he was going to call in a few days. In the meantime, we need to find out how we're going to pull it off."

"Are you saying you're going to do it?" Sade's voice trembled.

Dolo just looked at her, and she read between the lines.

"So you're going to give him me and Chadijah just like that, are you serious?" She was starting to get hysterical.

"He didn't say anything about Chadijah, just you," Dolo said flatly.

Samantha was watching them go back and forth, taking it in. She couldn't really give two fucks about the whole ordeal; all she wanted was her grandma back safely.

"Well, I'm not doing it!" Sade glared at Dolo defiantly. Dolo and Samantha both looked at each other and pulled their guns simultaneously and said: "Yes, the fuck you are!"

Chapter 23

One thing Dolo and Samantha agreed on was that they had to get Nah-Nah back safely by any means. Sade wasn't willing to trade her life for Nah-Nah's, but at the moment she didn't have a choice. Dolo and Samantha were holding her at Dolo's house. "We need to come up with another plan because trading me for Nah-Nah is only going to be temporary solution. Y'all don't know Abu. After he gets me, he's still going to come for you. The only upper hand we have right now is that he doesn't know about Samantha!" Sade said.

Dolo looked over at Samantha as if seeing her for the first time. Samantha was 5'7", coffee-colored, and she was thicker than Sade a little bit. If you stood the three of them side by side, you could tell that they were siblings. "Samantha, how did you learn about the contract on us?" Dolo asked her; he had yet to pick her brains.

"It's a website on the dark web that I go to get my contacts I've been doing this since I was in the military. I served nine years in the army. I was a Delta Force operator. They trained me to kill. I hold the record for verified kills. My specialty is with the sniper rifle."

"Wait a minute," Dolo thought on it. "That was you atop of the YMCA that day?" Dolo inquired.

Samantha grinned and said: "Yea, here's what I don't understand. How y'all kept getting away. Maybe it just means for me to kill y'all because I really don't miss. Like that night I was dressed up like a cop. I shot point-blank range into your car and didn't hit either of you. Shit like that hardly happens."

"That's why we're supposed to be on the same side but instead y'all are trying to get a baby sister killed," Sade spoke up.

"Man, quit crying! We're not going to really trade you but we're going to make Abu believe that we are. But we need a plan as to how we're going to trick him!" Dolo said.

Dolo and Samantha had discussed their options and had come to the conclusion that trading Sade wasn't it. Plus, they knew their grandmother wouldn't approve of it. Once they find out where the swap was supposed to take place, they would be able to put a game plan together.

"Well, y'all could've fooled me," Sade said, pouting.

"Look, Samantha," Dolo started, "where do we stand? Are you going to let the beef go that you have with our mom or what? Because I can't be watching my front while having to worry about you shooting me in the back."

"Yah, I'm over it. Like Sade said, the stuff with your mom has nothing to do what y'all."

"Good. Sade, what else do you know that can be of some help because until we meet him I'm gonna be on his ass."

"He has two accountants that handle all of his finances. One lives in Saudi Arabia and the other one resides in New York City,"

"New York City, here I come."

A text came through on Dolo's phone, catching his attention.

Oshun: *Dolo I need to talk to you*

Dolo: *Nay, you good. We ain't got shit to talk about*

Oshun: *It's important*

"Get me his address and I'll be back later," Dolo shrugged into his jacket.

"Where are you going?" Sade questioned.

"I gotta go holler at somebody real quick—Y'all need some girl time anyway," he said and walked out. Dolo climbed into the F-150 rental and swerved.

Dolo wondered what was so important that Oshun couldn't tell him over the phone. Dolo pulled in *Fat Daddy's* and parked where he could see the whole parking lot. After about five minutes, Dolo saw Oshun's green Corvette ZR1 pull into the parking lot. He watched her park and get out. Dolo slowly shook his head from side to side. Oshun had on some black jeans that made her butt look higher. Dolo rolled his window down and called her name. She looked, turned around and started walking his way. Dolo got out and leaned up against the truck.

"Now what was so important?" he asked her.

"First, I want to apologize for the way I acted the other night, you didn't deserve that. But the real reason I wanted to talk to you was to let you know that someone had a twenty million-dollar bounty on your head. Face was contemplating collecting it and he asked us what we wanted to do. My brother was trying to do it but I told them hell no. They tend to listen to me. See, Face doesn't really need the money. He owns a bunch of clubs and strip clubs. And we don't really need it either; we do shit to feed the team. I told them you had never crossed us, and Face is big on loyalty."

Twenty million isn't even half of the real bounty, Dolo thought to himself.

"I need you to find out who it was that came to Face with the idea."

"I'll try it. It's going to cost you."

"What?"

"You have to take me wherever you were going to take me that night I ran off."

Dolo contemplated leaving her where she stood but he reconsidered.

"Come on," Dolo grabbed her hand and led her to the passenger side.

He helped Oshun up into the truck, but unlike the last time, he didn't grab her butt. Dolo got in as Oshun was plugging her phone up. She cut on GloRilla's new mixtape and looked at Dolo.

"What, girl?"

"Nothing, I was just going to see if you were going to say something about me cutting GloRilla on," she admitted.

"I fuck with shorty the long way. She be saying shit which a regular bitch is scared to say. What have you been up to lately besides causing trouble?"

She shrugged. "Not too much, really. I be chilling until I'm not." Dolo chuckled, looking at her from head to toe. She had her hair in two long braids that fell to the middle of her back. There was a touch of lip gloss on her full lips, making them much more kissable. And the tight long-sleeved shirt she was wearing showcased the fact that she didn't have a stomach.

"Eyes on the road, I ain't trying to die in a car crash," she caught him staring.

"And how do you want to die?"

"With my knife in my hand," she said, making Dolo look over at her again.

"You crazy as hell." Dolo shook his head.

"Not nearly as crazy as you," Oshun said, leaning her seat back and closing her eyes.

Dolo got on I-95 and floored the F-150. Oshun didn't know that he was taking her to the beach. The night that he originally planned to take her to the beach, he was planning on trying to fuck her but now it was just to chill. He cracked the window, letting some night air into the truck. Immediately, Dolo saw Oshun's nipples get hard.

"You're trying to freeze me to death," Oshun crossed her arms over her chest.

Dolo rolled the window up and cut the cruise control on. After about ten minutes, Oshun started snoring softly. Dolo lost himself in his thoughts. After he killed Abu, he was going on a six-month vacation. Dolo was always the one on the offensive. Never before had he had to play defense. He didn't really even know how to play defense; it was so foreign to him.

They pulled into Myrtle Beach an hour later. Dolo parked at the Hampton Inn and woke Oshun up.

"Come on, woman" Dolo slapped her on the thigh.

"Where are we?" Oshun rubbed her yes.

"The beach, now come on!" Dolo got out.

Oshun hopped out of the truck and followed Dolo. They walked to the shore and stood there watching the waves crash into the shore.

"Why did you want to come to the beach?" Dolo wondered.

"The serenity of it. It gives me a sense of calm. I've only been to the beach one other time. My life is so chaotic that I never really get any downtime. Every time I turn around, it's something." She hugged herself as the breeze came off the ocean.

"You must be very cold." Dolo took his coat off and tried to hand it to her.

"What are you going to wear? No, I've got a better idea." She grabbed Dolo and pulled him down, and then climbed in his lap, catching him off guard. She wrapped them both inside the coat and continued watching the waves.

"Oshun, you wild as hell." He chuckled, wrapping his arms around her.

Oshun's butter-soft ass caused Dolo's manhood to rock up. Oshun felt it and looked up at him.

"You wanna fuck me, Dolo?" she asked softly, looking him in the eye.

Dolo didn't know how to respond. The way she asked him was just so sexy that he leaned down and kissed her. Their tongues started to dance and Oshun leaned back, pulling Dolo with her.

"Are you sure?" Dolo asked, breaking the kiss. Oshun nodded. "Yes."

"Come on." Dolo helped her up.

They went inside the hotel and got a penthouse suite. Dolo was unable to keep his hands off of Oshun. The whole elevator ride, they were feeling each other up. Everything on her was soft! Dolo got Oshun in the suite and carried her to the king-sized bed. He pulled his shirt over his head and unbuckled his belt, letting his jeans fall to the floor. Dolo looked down at Oshun; she lay back on the bed, grinning. Oshun's chocolate ass was looking too fucking good to describe. He climbed on top of the bed before making his way down and sucking on her neck.

"Mm," she moaned as he put hickies all over her neck.

Dolo pulled her shirt over her head and unclasped her bra, revealing her melon-sized breasts. Dolo took one of her nipples into his mouth while unzipping her jeans.

"Doolooo!" Oshun moaned, grabbing the back of his head.

He pulled the rest of her clothes down and the knives fell out. Dolo pushed them aside on the bed and pulled the thong she had on down her legs. Oshun's pussy was so phat that it stood out from between her legs about three inches. Dolo kissed her pussy lips, making Oshun jump. Dolo sucked her clit into his mouth, and the door flew off the hinges. Before Dolo could get to his gun, somebody kicked him in the back of the head and kicked him sideways. The next thing he knew, he was getting kicked and punched. Dolo caught someone's leg by the ankle and pushed their knee with his palm, breaking their knee. "Move!" someone yelled

Dolo looked up through the sea of bodies and saw Sayyid bringing a gun down his way before blacking out.

Chapter 24

When Dolo woke up, he was suspended in the air by his arms by a car chain. The agony in his shoulders were sending jolts of pain through his upper body. He looked around and saw he was in an empty basement that had seen much use. Dust coated the floor and spider webs were all over the basement. Dolo looked and saw Oshun in the corner tied to a steel pipe.

"Oshun!" he yelled, causing his body to swing a little bit, making the pain in his shoulder ignite.

"You need to stop making all that noise before they come back down here," Oshun muttered.

"Are you okay?

"Why would I be? I'm sure I would've gotten away but then I wouldn't have known where to find you," she said, trying to get the cuffs off.

"So you know where we're at?"

"Yes, they think that I'm a child. Their guard was completely let down around me. They didn't even search me, which is going to be a fatal mistake." Dolo thought about the knives that had fallen out of her clothes. "They drove us to Charlotte—we're in the basement of a mega mansion," Oshun informed him.

Dolo looked around the basement again. There wasn't anything out of the ordinary, but then Dolo saw the drain in the middle of the floor. Then he saw the dark stains on the floor around him. Dolo knew from experience that the dark stains on the floor were blood, and the drain in the middle of the floor was where they let the blood run into.

They were basically in a torture chamber of some kind. Dolo knew they had to get out of there immediately. He tried loosening the chains around his wrists and sent sharp pains through his shoulder. His shoulder felt like they were about to come of the socket. Footsteps drew their attention to the steps. The first thing Dolo saw were a pair of white Italian loafers followed by several pairs of boots. The body that came down the stairs that were in the loafers was none other than Abu. He had an air about him that yelled power, arrogance and money all in one. Abu strolled over to Dolo like he didn't want the bottom of his loafers to touch the ground. He walked up to Dolo until they were face to face and grinned, showing off a set of perfect white teeth.

"Funny seeing you here," Abu said in a thick accent, walking out of Dolo's sight.

The boots belonged to Sayyid and two other desert fatigue-clad Arabs with hard faces.

"The last time we conversed, you said something along the lines of I was going to die with pork chop in my mouth," Abu stepped back into Dolo's line of vision.

Dolo sized Abu up. Abu was six feet seven, a fit one-eighty, with low cut hair and a full beard. Abu was darker than other Arabs that Dolo was used to seeing, and he had real bushy eyebrows over a pair of hazel eyes. Abu didn't have the face of a hardened soldier; he was more of a privileged little boy.

"The offer still stands, I can have the pork chop cooked and in your dead mouth in an hour. Ummph!" Dolo forcefully released his breath. Then, Sayyid kicked him in the stomach, making him swing. Dolo had to grit his teeth to bite back a yell. His arms and shoulders felt like they were on fire.

"Tsk! Tsk! Tsk! You're not smart at all. Don't you see you're at a disadvantage? But if you would let me know where I can find Sade, I'll allow you to retain your life, both arms and one leg," Abu said smugly and one of the fatigue-clad soldiers pulled out a new machete.

"What do you take me for? A fool? You get your hands on Sade and see if I don't make it out of this basement with breath in my body. So, come with a better proposition, pig!" Dolo spat. One of the soldiers stepped up to hit Dolo, but Dolo was anticipating the move. Dolo kicked his feet up, catching the soldier in the throat, crushing his windpipe. When Dolo's feet came back down, both his shoulders were dislocated. Then, Sayyid and the remaining soldier started punching and kicking him with his hands still suspended in the air above his head. Dolo was forced to endure the beating.

"Okay, that's enough," Abu said after five minutes of Dolo getting beaten.

One of Dolo's eyes were swollen shut; his face was purple from bruising, and he had a few broken ribs.

"Are you ready to tell me where Sade is or do I need to allow them to continue the beating?" Abu questioned Dolo.

"Fuck you," Dolo mumbled real low so that Abu had to strain to hear him.

"What was that?" Abu got closer, and Dolo spat in his face. Abu wiped the spit out of his face frantically.

"Stop!" Oshun yelled from across the room, causing everyone to look her way.

They had all but forgot about her.

"I can get you Sade but you have to stop hitting him."

"Is that right? And how can you do that?" Abu inquired, walking in Oshun's direction.

"By bringing her to you," Oshun grinned.

"What's so funny?" Abu questioned, standing in front of her.

"How stupid you are," she laughed and threw one of her knives, stabbing him in the stomach.

112

The other soldier rushed in Oshun's direction, earning him a knife in the throat. Sayyid stood by Abu's side as he doubled over in pain

"Come on! We need to get you to the hospital," Sayyid said. Then, shooting daggers at Oshun with his eyes, Sayyid said: "You'll die a painful death when I return!"

Sayyid helped Abu up the stairs, leaving Oshun with an unconscious Dolo.

Kah! Kah! Boc! Boc! Boom! Gunfire erupted upstairs in the house. Then several feet were heard down the steps.

"Ogun!" Oshun yelled, seeing him rush down the step. Oshun knew it was only a matter of time before he met her. Oshun and Ogun both had apps on their phone where they could pinpoint each other's location.

"Are you okay?" Ogun rushed to Oshun and started trying to feel her.

Ogun shot the handcuffs, loosening Oshun from the pipe. She immediately rushed over to Dolo and started trying to the free him. Ogun looked at her like she was crazy.

"He's the reason you were even in this position!" Ogun said, but Oshun ignored him.

Oshun found the lever on the wall that the chain was tied to and released it, sending Dolo to the ground, making him regain consciousness.

"Come on, we need to go!" Oshun tried to help him up.

With both of Dolo's shoulders dislocated, he was in excruciating pain.

"Wait, wait. You need to pop my shoulder back in place. Grab my wrist and upper arm and push it up into the socket. It's going to make a popping noise." Dolo instructed her on what to do.

Oshun did as instructed and popped both of Dolo's shoulders back in place. The pain eased tremendously.

"Where is Abu?" Dolo questioned.

"They got away in a black Range Rover," Ogun said. Dolo shook his head and got woozy. He needed to get some rest. The beating that he'd taken had him drained and broken. Dolo could barely see out of his eyes. His nose was broken, his face was swollen like the Elephant Man's, and he felt like a few of his ribs were broken. Oshun helped Dolo outside to a car and got in, followed by TNT.

"Take us to the house," Oshun said.

"Oshun, are you serious right now? You're gonna put yourself in harm's way for him again? What are you going to do if they find y'all again? He can't even defend himself right now," Ogun reasoned.

"The army wouldn't stand a chance against me at my house and you know. So, take me the fuck home!" She had her mind made up.

Dolo could speak his peace but he didn't want to put any more of a rift between the two siblings, so he just laid calm and let them handle it.

"Put four cars outside of her house. If anything happens to my sister, y'all can go ahead and kill yourselves," Ogun told them and walked off.

Chapter 25

Oshun was going to make someone a happy wife one day. The entire three days that Dolo had been at her house, she had suffocated him. If Dolo was in the market for a girlfriend, Oshun would definitely be number one on his list. She tended to his every need; she even showed Dolo a submissive side that he never knew she had. Dolo had talked to Sade and Samantha and let them know what was going on and where they were so they wouldn't be worried.

Oshun had a two-story house across the river that sat in a cul-de-sac. So Oshun could see someone the minute they turned down her street. The Cape Fear River was behind her house, and she definitely wasn't worried about someone coming from that direction. Oshun kept at least three Tiaras with her the whole three days that Dolo was there. Oshun made it clear by her actions that Dolo was off limits. Oshun stayed with Dolo all the way. If she wasn't trying to tend to his injuries or feed him, then she'd just hang around, sitting in his lap. Ogun had made just one appearance to Oshun's house since Dolo was brought here. Dolo had to admit that he liked the little set-up. It wasn't as good as his house, but her spot was a nice little safe zone.

"You ready to leave now that you're all healed up?" Casey's thick caramel ass said.

Casey was Oshun's second-in-command; she'd been at Oshun's spot the empire time that Dolo was there. Casey was an extra thick, twenty-year-old caramel-skinned beauty. Her body was like that of Doja Cat and her face was like that of Ruby Rose. Casey was cool as fuck and down to earth, but Oshun said that Casey was one of her most ruthless Tiaras.

"I got shit to do and people to see. And I got a score that needs to be settled," Dolo said back. Dolo had been laying back the entire three days trying to figure out who it was that had approached Face about the bounty on their heads. More importantly, he wanted to know how they had gotten him in the first place. And he hadn't told anyone where he was headed other night. And for Sayyid to be the one who had found him was a real problem. They could've just sent one of their suicide bombers into the room and be done with it, but they had fucked up. Abu had knocked a hornet's nest down, and he had nowhere to run.

What was even better was that Dolo knew Abu had to get in contact with him in order to try and get Sade.

"You going somewhere?" Oshun's short ass walked in the living room in a silk, hot pink pajama short set that was two sizes too small.

The shorts were so tight that they were tucked into her sex lips.

"It's time for me to get back to it. This nigga Abu probably knows by now that we got away, so he's gonna be calling me soon. And I need to be ready for him when he does. I have to make sure I'm properly prepared." Dolo winked as he pulled his hoodie over his head.

The swelling in Dolo's face had gone down, but his ribs still felt sore.

"You know I'm coming with you, right?" Oshun stood with her hand on her hips.

"No. What you're going to do is find out that information for me like I asked you. And be ready for me when I slide black though because we need to finish what we started."

Oshun smiled a big Kool-Aid smile because she knew he was referring to them fucking. Dolo hadn't been able to fuck Oshun yet, but he was going to.

"Whatever," she continued to grin.

"Drop me off real quick so I can go ahead and handle my business then I can get back here and fuck your brains out."

"Eweee! Too much info, thank you," Casey said.

"Close your ears then." Oshun rolled her eyes. "Let me go throw something on right quick."

While Oshun went to put something on, Dolo called Melissa and told her to meet him at his house. Then he called Jigga.

"Back from the dead," Jigga joked, answering his phone.

"Nigga, I don't know what death tastes like but when I do, it's not gonna be at the hands of no Arab, brother!" Dolo boasted.

"Glad to hear you're still the same, Dolo, and you didn't let your brush with death change your attitude. What is happening though? What kind of hell do you have brewing? And I know you so you can't tell me that you don't have some recent smoke up."

Dolo cracked a smile because Jigga knew him like the back of his hand.

"You know I'm gonna make Abu feel like shit. I'm just touching base with you to let you know I'm good but I'm sure Sade already told Melissa to tell you what happened."

"Yea, I was informed. What do you need me to do?"

"Nothing at the moment. Just stand by."

Oshun and Casey walked back in the room as Dolo was ending the call.

"Talking to your lady?" Casey asked, making Oshun narrow her eyes.

Dolo started to say something slick but his mind was on some bullshit, so he bit his tongue. He would check her on a later date; right now, he had to set someone up a date with the Grim Reaper.

They sensed his mood because they didn't say anything else. Oshun and Dolo got in her Vette with Casey trailing behind them in a red Track Hawk.

"Handle what you need to handle and call me," Oshun said before dropping Dolo off at his house. He nodded and got out; he had business to attend to.

Chapter 26

When Dolo walked into the house, Sade, Samantha and Melissa had somber looks on her faces.

"Why are y'all looking like that?" Dolo asked, reaching down and petting Simba and Sasha's heads.

Sade got up, walked over to Dolo and handed him her phone. Dolo looked at the phone and dropped it. The phone landed on its back, spider-webbing the screen, but the picture of Nah-Nah on the ground—bloody and swollen—would forever be burned in Dolo's brain. Under the picture was the caption: *You'll never get her back. You're next.* Sadness, pain and rage were the feelings coursing through Dolo's body in that order. He didn't want to just kill Abu; he wanted to torture him until he died, to bring him back and to do it all over again. The ache Dolo was feeling in his chest was unbearable. The loss of Nah-Nah was too much! Dolo turned around and walked back out of the house, grabbing his keys. He climbed into his Camaro and was getting ready to pull off when Melissa knocked on the passenger side window. Dolo was going to ignore her and pull off because he wanted to be alone. However, he unlocked the door and she climbed in.

"Where you're going, I'm going too!" Melissa declared. Dolo knew how stubborn she could be and he wasn't in the mood to argue, so he went ahead and pulled off. With no set destination, Dolo cruised around the city. Dolo was so mad he couldn't think straight; sensing this, Melissa said:

"Focus, nigga! Don't let your emotions cloud your judgment. I can't pretend to know how you're feeling because I've never been in your shoes. Channel that shit and let somebody feel the same way you're feeling. I don't care who it is!" Melissa's words were ringing true. Melissa knew Dolo, so she knew how he was when he got in his moods. She left him alone and started texting Sade. Dolo was trying to figure out how he was going to go at Abu next, but he couldn't get his mind to do what he needed it to do.

"Drive here," Melissa put the address into the car's GPS.

"Why? Who's there?" Dolo said the first words he'd spoken since coming out the house.

"Abu's second wife and two daughters."

Dolo floored the Camaro. He was about to do them something dirty! This was just what Dolo needed to get mind right.

"How did you find this out?"

"Sade sent it to me. She said she was on his uncle's laptop trying to gather some more intel and ran across the address." Dolo looked at the address and saw it was in Cary, North Carolina. Cary was in the top three of the safest cities in the U.S. It wasn't making sense to Dolo because if he had two daughters by the woman, then Sade's daughter was Abu's only child. Dolo didn't give a fuck one way or the other. When he got down, Chadijah would be Abu's only child.

"I'ma 'bout to see just how deep your savage run," Dolo said to Melissa.

"Deeper than yours," she shot back.

They got to Cary an hour later. They pulled up outside of a nice three-story house twenty minutes after that. Dolo didn't give this action any thought. He was more than sure that if this was really one of Abu's wives, then she had some sort of security team but with the loss of Nah-Nah, he could care less. As soon as he and Melissa exited the car and started approaching the house, four Arabs came out of nowhere speaking Arabic. Dolo and Melissa both upped at the same time, gunning them down. Dolo never broke his stride; he proceeded to the front door and kicked it off the hinges. Dolo took the first floor and Melissa went up the steps two at a time. Two Arabs were sitting in the living room. Dolo sat them both down permanently with shots to the dome. Dolo had just cleared the first floor when heard Melissa's hammer bark three times. He rushed up the stairs and found Melissa standing over two more Arabs. Then, they went to the third floor together. They rushed into the master bedroom and saw an Arab ushering a woman and two girls into what appeared to be a closet. Melissa shot him in the back of head, spraying the woman with brain matter and skull fragments.

"Aah!" she yelled, slamming the door shut.

The way the door shut, Dolo knew it wasn't a regular door; it was steel. Then Melissa pointed at the keypad by the handle. Dolo had been hearing about panic rooms for a while but this was his first time actually encountering one. He knew you couldn't break into them nor burn them down, but he had an idea on how to get them to come out.

"Come on," Dolo said. "Do you have a lighter?"

"Yea, why?"

"Let me see it."

Dolo went into the hallway and pulled the ladder down that led to the attic. Dolo climbed up in the attic, lit the insulation on fire in the corners and scrambled back down the ladder.

"Let's go outside and wait," Dolo said.

They walked outside and sat on the hood of Dolo's car. The roof of the house was ablaze. Dolo knew the smoke was going to flush them out of the panic room and right into his arms.

They didn't have to wait long; the woman and two girls came stumbling out of the house coughing. Melissa snatched the two girls up and put them in the backseat of the Camaro. Dolo roughly grabbed the woman by the back of her neck and tossed her in the truck.

"Hey, man! What are you doing?" a heavy-set white man questioned, walking in Dolo's direction.

"Minding your business is something you might want to do," Dolo warned him.

"Get that woman out of that trunk or I'm calling the—"

Boom! His head snapped back and he crumpled to the ground.

"Let's go!" Melisasa screamed, holding a smoking gun. Dolo got into the car and they made their way back to Fayetteville. Dolo looked in the rearview mirror at the girls. One was about thirteen and the other one was no more than six. They we huddled together in the backseat; he could smell the fear coming off of them. Dolo pulled into his gate and drove around back to the gator pen. It had been a while since he'd fed them, so he knew they were starving. Dolo got out and popped the trunk.

"Get your stupid ass out!" he yelled and the woman started speaking fast in Arabic.

The hijab she was wearing only revealed her gray eyes. Dolo snatched the hijab off. She was drop-dead gorgeous! He grabbed a handful of her long black hair and yanked her out of the trunk and onto the ground. Sade and Samantha came walking up with both chow-chows as Melissa got the little girls out of the Camaro. When the woman saw Sade, she narrowed her eyes and started talking rapidly in Arabic. After going back and forth in Arabic, the woman sneered at Sade and spat at her feet. Sade pulled her gun out and shot her in the leg. Everyone but the two daughters smiled.

"What she say, sis?" Samantha wanted to know.

"That I was going to be like my grandmother real soon."

"Sade, record this so you can post it," Dolo said, pulling a ski mask over his bald head.

Dolo grabbed the smaller daughter up and carried her into the gator pen. Dolo didn't see any of the gators, so he knew they were all in the water. He walked about four feet from the bank and turned towards Sade.

"Abu! You are the reason the young child has to die. You stole something very dear to me and now I plan to repay you tenfold." Dolo glared at the iPhone.

Dolo grabbed the girl's hands and swung her around in a circle, and she started giggling, enjoying the circular motion, thinking he was playing with her. Once Dolo felt like he had enough speed, he let go and sent her sailing out into the pond. As soon as she hit the water, all the gators started swimming and her direction. The first one next to her took her little head off. Her mother started screaming and yelling. Dolo went over and stopped by the other girl.

"Watch 'em! Watch 'em!" Dolo said, and Simba and Sasha started growling at her. "Get 'em!"

The chow-chows charged at her at the same time. Simba jumped in the air and they hit her in sync. Simba hit her high, taking a chunk out of the middle of her chest, and Sasha hit her low, tearing a piece of her muscle off. She crumpled to the ground, grabbing her wounds. Then, Sasha pounced at her face, sinking her teeth into the girl's neck, killing her. Then the camera tuned to Abu's wife where Samantha had her on her knees, grabbing a handful of hair.

"Abu, you're next," Samantha said and swung the machete she had in the other hand, cutting Abu's wife's head off.

Samantha tossed her head in the air and the camera followed it until it landed in the pond where it was immediately grabbed by one of the smaller gators. They had sent a major statement.

Chapter 27

Dolo was keeping the pressure on. After he fed the gators, he changed clothes. Then, he and Melissa went on a plane to New York City. Dolo was on the way to take Abu's accountant out of the game. Dolo's phone started ringing the minute they grabbed their bags from baggage claim.

"Yea," he answered.

"I've just seen on the internet where his accountant is set to be at a black tie gala on the bottom floor of the Trump Hotel," Sade said.

"Okay, where are you at?" Dolo asked because it sounded like he heard a loud speaker in the background.

"About to board a plane with Samantha to Las Vegas."

Dolo wasn't feeling it but there was nothing he could do about it now, plus she was with Samantha. So, he knew Sade was going to be okay. Dolo ended the call. He and Melissa caught a taxi to the Trump Hotel.

"So how are we going to get him?" Melissa asked, turning to face Dolo.

"We're going to go to his black tie event and you're going to put a few drops of *this* into his drink. Initially we were going to find a way to inject him with it but this way is even better."

"What is it?" Melissa grabbed the bottle out of Dolo's hand.

"It's just from a mushroom called *Amanita Virosa*. A few drops will shut a person's kidney down, resulting in immediate death."

"And how am I supposed get it into his drink?" she inquired and Dolo smirked.

"Just trust me."

They pulled into the Trump Hotel and Dolo paid cash for a suite with two beds. They put their bags in the suite and left right back out. Time was of the essence. They only had three hours to grab the stuff required to succeed in killing Abu's accountant—George Kaza. They rode the elevator downstairs to the library.

"Excuse me but what kind of event are you having tonight?" Dolo stopped a staffer of the hotel.

"A black tie gala for some foreign ambassadors. If I were you I'd get settled in my room before it actually starts because once it does, security is going to be so tight you won't be able to sneeze without security harassing you."

"Okay, thanks," Dolo said.

Dolo and Melissa sat down in the lobby and watched as security walked K-9's through, sniffing for explosives. It was then that Dolo saw one of the waitresses disappear down a side hallway.

"Go ahead back to the room. I'll be there shortly."

"What are you about to do?" Melissa didn't want to leave him by himself.

"I'm good—I should be up in about five minutes," he reassured her.

Melissa went to the elevator while Dolo disappeared down the side hallway. Dolo found a uniform that would fit Melissa and folded it over his arm. He made it back to the suite and tossed the uniform on the bed.

"Melissa!" Dolo called out.

"Yea! I'm in the bathroom." Melissa was in the spa tub filled with bubbles. The tub was big enough to hold four people.

"Okay, this is the game plan." Dolo started. "I got you a waitress uniform. All you have to do is take the drinks to his table and allow me to do the rest."

"Well, I got two hours until show time. Come relax with me. The sensation in this tub is like you're getting a massage." She leaned her head back, enjoying the feeling.

Dolo was too wound up to relax; he was focused on crippling Abu before he had a chance of strike back.

Reading his mind, Melissa said, "Nigga, you're better to me and yourself when you relaxed and have a clear mind. This tub will do it, get in!" she demanded.

Dolo shook his head, stripped down to his Tommy briefs and was about to get in when she said:

"Boy, take them off. You ain't got shit I ain't never seen nor heard before."

Dolo took them off and climbed into the tub.

"Shit!" Dolo said, sinking down into the tub. The hot water started soothing his body, taking all of the tenseness out of his muscles. He rested his head back against the edge of the tub and closed his eyes. *I need this*, he thought to himself.

"You know what else would help you?" Melissa asked.

"What?" Dolo questioned, his eyes still closed.

"This," she reached under the water and started massaging Dolo's pole.

He wanted to protest but he was backed up and her hands felt like heaven. Dolo opened his eyes and looked at Melissa. The upper half of her body was out of the water, showcasing her upturned C-cups. Instinctively, Dolo leaned forward and took one of her nipples into his mouth.

"Mm," she moaned.

Dolo circled her nipple with his tongue, making her eyes roll into the back of her head. Dolo stood up, breaking her grip on his swollen manhood and sat her on the edge of the tub. Melissa's golden-brown skin glowed in the dimly lit room. Dolo got down between her legs and sucked her love button into his warm mouth, sending waves of pleasure through her body. Locking her clit in his mouth, Dolo used his thumb to massage her back door. "Dolooo!" she yelled as her orgasm started coming up from the bottom of her feet.

They knew what the other one liked and disliked. Dolo put his thumb in her butt and flicked his tongue up and down her button, causing her to drench his face with her love potion. Dolo had to hold her to keep her from falling on the floor. Once he got her steady, he got out of the tub, stood at the edge and turned her around. She was still sitting on the edge of the tub, but now Dolo was standing between her legs. His dick was already standing at attention and she was dripping wet, so he was able to slide right in.

"Damn, this shit tight, Melissa!" Dolo groaned, gripping her shapely hips.

Melissa wrapped her arms around him in a forward motion.

"You—trying to make—me nut," he said, trying to concentrate on not busting a nut before she did.

"Grr!" Dolo picked her up and carried her to one of the beds.

He pinned both of Melissa's legs up to her head and started to hit her with long, hard, fast strokes.

"Unn! Unn! Unn!" she moaned, reaching her hand down and playing with her sex button.

"This is still my pussy!" Dolo sped up more.

"Dolooo!" Melissa moaned and coated Dolo's pipe with juices.

Dolo was able to get five more pumps in before he sprayed her insides with his seed. He collapsed on top of her and fell asleep. They had an hour until show time.

Chapter 28

Sade and Samantha's plane touched down at Las Vegas International at 5 o'clock in the evening. Compared to Dolo and Melissa's moves, Samantha had a few connections that got them everything they needed and some. She had gotten a room for herself and Sade right across the street from the Coliseum, which was where the money convention was being held. With time to kill, Sade and Samantha went to the spa and got pampered.

"As I think about it you're a mentally strong individual," Sade told Samantha as she watched the nail tech clean her cuticle.

"What makes you say that?" Samantha grinned.

"Because you're sitting here getting a mani and pedicure, having girl talk like you're not going to do what you're about to do," Sade said in a coded way so that the nail tech, who she knew was listening, wouldn't be able to tell anything.

"Sis, I'm numb to it, I compartmentalize extremely good. Let's not talk about that. I want to know how you got involved with someone like Abu." Samantha took the spot off herself.

"Where do I begin? I was a cleaning lady. For his company building in Charlotte and he came to town. I was a low level employee. I didn't even know who he was. One day he came to Charlotte to discuss business with his uncle and that was our first time meeting. He swept me off my feet literally, girl! He picked me up and carried me to his

Phantom the first time he laid eyes on me. He wined and dined me to death. And you've never met him but he had this aura about him that I can't explain." Sade looked off dreamily.

"You don't have to explain. I understand totally. I've encountered my share of boss niggas, so I can only imagine what Abu is like. Because not only is he a boss but he's a prince of a whole country."

"After that we had a whirlwind romance, he spoiled me, fucked me and put a baby in me, all in that order. But after I got pregnant, I started seeing his true colors. He began to be abusive and controlling, then I learned about his illicit affairs and started to distance myself from him. He got wind of it and threatened my life. He showed me videos of what Sayyid did to people who went against him. That's when I made copies of anything I could and fled. Now here I am." Sade's voice was laced with pain.

"What about his father, the king?"

"He's a gentle soul but I could sense an underlying bit of malice in him too though."

"You don't get to be in his position without it," Samantha added.

"Whew!" Samantha stretched her limbs and stood up. The nail techs had done their thing! Samantha had gotten two ice pick coffin nails with smiley faces on her trigger fingers. Sade had gotten coffin nails too, except hers were powder blue with diamonds on her ring fingers.

"Perfect timing. We have thirty minutes to get to the hotel and get set up," Sade said.

The plan was for Samantha to put her sniper skills to use. They had already used some glass cutter to cut a hole in their room window. Now all that was left to be done was set up the rifle and wait. Samantha was going to shoot Muhammed in the head before he made it inside the Coliseum. They got back to the hotel just as people started filing into the convention.

"Help me move this bed," Samantha said.

Sade and Samantha moved the bed over to the window, and Sade watched as Samantha put the sniper rifle together that Dolo had gotten from Jigga. Dolo didn't even know that they had taken it. By the time he found out, it would be too late. Samantha had it overnighted to Las Vegas. Samantha set up the rifle and looked through the nine-power scope "Sade, grab those binoculars on the table over there. I'm going to need you to spot him for me and I'll do the rest. After you tell me who he is, take our bags and go wait for me in the car. I already got us booked on the next flight!" Samantha said, adjusting the dials on the rifle.

"Okay."

Sade looked through the high-powered binoculars at all the people entering the Coliseum, trying to spot Abu's accountant. Then, it dawned on her that Muhammed was not just going to waltz into the convention. From her time around him, she knew he liked to be the center of attention. Sade looked further up the street and saw a convoy of cars coming up the street. In the middle of the convoy was a black limo with Saudi Arabian flags attached to the windows.

"The black limo coming up the street has to be him."

Sade followed the limo up the street until it stopped in front of the Coliseum. Sade looked down over at Samantha sprawled across the bed, peeking through scope with a dead smiley face on the trigger. Sade put the binoculars back up to her face as the limo doors opened, and the limo was swarmed by Arabs that Sade knew to be on Abu's personal security team.

"Tell me the second you see him and which door he's getting out of," Samantha said, keeping her focus on the doors.

Muhammed stepped out of the back passenger side in a blue and grey two-piece suit. "There he is—back door passenger side," Sade gave Samantha his description. Samantha turned the dial with the right clicks and took a slow breath, lining Muhammed's head up in her crosshairs. *Kaboom!* Samantha put Muhammed's brains all over the Coliseum steps.

"Move! Move! Let's go!" Samantha yelled, breaking the rifle down.

Sade scrambled out the door and to the elevator, keeping her face shielded from the cameras Samantha wiped everything down, everything they'd touched in thirty seconds flat and was out of the room. She also kept her face shielded as she descended the steps with the rifle slung over the shoulder. Samantha rushed down the seven flights and was walking up to their rental car as Sade crunk it up. Sade took off before Samantha could close the door. They got to Las Vegas International and were on a flight back across the country all before the coroner got Muhammed's body to the morgue.

Chapter 29

Melissa fit the uniform Dolo had stolen perfectly. It was the perfect blend of *professional* and *sexy*, making it easy for her to be incognito.

"Listen, once you give his table the drinks, walk out the front door and I'll be there waiting for you." Dolo swatted her on the ass and walked out. He'd just gotten the text from Sade that Muhammed was no longer amongst the living. Dolo was secretly proud of them; they'd made his work easier. Dolo went and sat inside the rental and waited for Melissa to do her thing. Melissa checked the room one more time, making sure they had not left anything, and stepped out. She got downstairs to the lobby and blended into the crowd. No one gave her a second glance when she stepped out on the ballroom floor. Melissa spotted George at a table in the front with three other people. George was a tall, middle-aged white man with liver spots on his hands and head. Melissa made her way straight to his table.

"Hi! Is there anything I can get you?" Melissa smiled.

"Actually you can. Can you get us a bottle of your best white wine?" the white lady sitting on George's right requested.

"Honey, you know I don't drink," George said.

He had a squeaky nasal voice.

"Tonight you do."

Melissa walked off in the direction she'd seen all the staff walk.

"Hey, I just started. Where do I get bottles of wine?" Melissa asked a chubby white girl.

"I get it. What kind do they want?" she inquired.

"They said they want the best white wine we have." Melissa relayed the message.

"Okay, wait here."

While she went to go get the wine, Melissa texted Dolo and told him she would be out in less than five minutes.

"We ran out of white, so this is on in the house," she handed Melissa the bottle.

"Okay," Melissa smiled.

Melissa took the bottle to George's table and grabbed everyone's glasses. With no one paying her any attention, Melissa was able to squeeze a few drops of the lethal poison in George's glass. He made a toast, and they all downed the wine. Melissa walked out; she didn't need to see anymore when she got outside. Dolo was parked at the curb. They hadn't got a block down the road when ambulances started shooting past them. They looked at each other and smiled.

***

"Nigga, you not shit!" Oshun snapped on Dolo. "You ain't call, you ain't do shit. I'm sitting around waiting to hear from you and I don't even get a call letting me know nothing!" she narrowed her eyes.

Dolo was sitting on Oshun's couch, smirking at her while she vented. He swore he could see her dark chocolate skin turning red.

"Something funny?" Oshun swung on him.

Dolo blocked it, wrapped her up, and pulled her down on his lap.

"Calm your sexy ass down. You know I got shit going on right now. Something came up that I had to handle." The smile left Dolo's face as he thought about Nah-Nah.

Seeing his mood change, Oshun asked him: "What happened?"

"Someone killed my granny."

"Sorry about that."

"Yea, chill and tell me what you've been up to."

"I've been chilling other than sending TNT and JBM on some missions to rob some dope spots. And we just hit for twenty bricks of heroin and ten bricks of cocaine."

"Shit! I might need to borrow some money," Dolo joked.

"How much?"

"You know I'm bullshitting." Dolo grabbed her butt, allowing his fingers to sink into the cheeks of her fleshy backside.

Dolo's phone rang, putting a pause on what he was about to do.

"What does it do?" he asked Jigga.

"Come by the spot real quick," Jigga said urgently.

"I'll be there in about twenty minutes." Dolo ended the call.

"Two more spots of mine got hit!" Jigga pounded his fist on the table. "But this time they fucked up. One of my workers was able to get away. It was those hellish TNT. I got a hundred thousand for every one of those motherfuckas you kill!" Jigga took a swig of tequila.

This was going to put Dolo in a tight spot. Oshun hadn't allowed Ogun and them to come for his neck, now it was his turn to return the favor. But Dolo knew how Jigga was; he wasn't going to be trying to hear shit.

"And I got five hundred million dollars' bounty on Face's head." Jigga sweetened the deal.

"Give me few days and let me see what I can come up with." Dolo stood up to leave.

"A'ight, do that."

They dapped up and Dolo left. Dolo didn't think he could do it and look himself in the mirror every day. He wasn't the type of nigga who went against his morals for some money, plus he wasn't hurting for no paper. Dolo looked down at his ringing phone and saw Ms. Shannon calling.

"Long time no talk to," Dolo answered.

"I should be saying that to you," she replied sassily, causing him to laugh.

"Let me find out I put this good D on you and now your ass is sprung," he said smugly.

"You coming over here?"

"Nope. I'm busy," he dismissed her.

"Sean, you have exactly thirty minutes to get here or I'ma cut up real bad."

"I'll be there in ten minutes," he chuckled and ended the call.

Dolo pulled up to Ms. Shannon's ten minutes later and hopped out. As he was walking up the steps, Shannon opened the door in a dark pink lingerie outfit.

"All this for me?" Dolo stepped in and cupped the bottom of one of her breasts.

"Depends," she swatted his hand away and walked away, making him follow her up the stairs.

"On what?"

"Oh how good you eat this pussy," she got on her bed and looked back.

"Picture that."

Dolo walked around to where her head was and pulled his wood out. She opened her mouth and welcomed his hard member with a flick of her tongue. Shannon swallowed him whole. She had the head of Dolo's dick down her throat, massaging his balls and humming all at the same time. Dolo only lasted five minutes before he emptied a family of his down her throat. Dolo fell over on the bed and drifted off.

"No you're not," Shannon protested, not wanting him to fall fast asleep. "You about to fuck me"

"Let me rest real quick," Dolo was halfway asleep.

"Boy, you on some shit." She shook her head. "Don't worry about it because you're gonna miss me when I'm gone!" she vowed.

"Woman, you ain't going to work."

"You a whole lie! I'm moving. I invested in some heroin with Jigga. I'm gonna clear an extra five million when it's done. The dope the Arabs have been hitting him with lately has been pure, let Jigga tell it. So he said he'll have it gone in—"

"Hold up, the dope—who has been hitting him, and why?" Dolo cut her off; he was wide awake now.

"Some Arab, why?" she saw the look on his face. "That shouldn't be anything new to you. Jigga's had an Arab plug since the very beginning." Dolo got up and dashed out of the house; he and Jigga had a lot to discuss.

Chapter 30

Jigga's plug was an Arab? That didn't make sense or did it? Dolo was thinking that it didn't make sense in the aspect of loyalty. Jigga was like a father to him. So there was no way he was fraternizing with enemy. There had to be a reasonable explanation. Ms. Shannon was probably tripping. Then, the devil was in his ear saying: *But what if Jigga was on some back door shit*? The more he thought on it, the more Dolo felt like the pieces fell into place. Before he made it to Jigga's house, he called Ms. Shannon.

"Are you sure Jigga's plug is an Arab?" Dolo needed her to be hundred percent sure.

"Yes! I know what the hell an Arab look like. I've only met him a few times and one of the times he told me he was from Saudi Arabia. Dolo, why does it matter so much?"

"I'll call you back." Dolo's mind was scrambled. What kind of shit did Jigga have going on? All the signs were pointing to Jigga being on some fuck shit. Dolo pulled up to Jigga's spot and got out. He strolled up to the front door and rang the bell. Jigga's maid answered the door.

"Where is Jigga?" he stepped inside.

"He went out of town about an hour ago. He told me he would be back next week sometime," she said.

Dolo did not respond; he walked back out of the house and got in his whip. He called Jigga.

"What up?" Jigga's voice boomed in his ear.

"Who is your plug?" Dolo got straight to the point.

"Huh? My plug? You tripping, you sound like one of them people."

"Nigga, don't fucking play me! I'm dead serious, who do you get your work from? Fuck all that sideways shit? I'm asking for a reason."

The phone went quiet like the call had dropped. Dolo had to pull it from his ear and look at that screen but it showed the call was still active.

"Hello," Dolo spoke.

"I've come to the conclusion that there are many different levels of love. Like I love you more than you could imagine, boy. But I love me and my money ten times more. I know it's a bad way for a person to feel about their child but it is what it is!" Jigga stated.

"Your child?"

"Dolo, why do you think I looked out for you the way I did when you were growing up? You and Sade are my kids. Your mother knew I was your pops; we just never voiced it. I know you don't believe me but I have the paternity test at the house to prove it. I'll text Clara and have her pull it out of the safe and bring it to you. Until then, to answer your questions, yes: Abu is my plug. I told your ass to leave the whole situation alone but you are so intent on collecting the bounty that you wouldn't listen. I didn't know it was Sade until you came to me. I tried countless times to see you but you kept digging yourself deeper. Now it's over and I can't allow your stupidity to mess up my cash flow."

"You're a whole bitch and a half! And fuck all that you're my father, and that makes you my enemy. That nigga killed Nah-Nah."

"So what! Motherfuckers die every day! I'm your enemy, big deal." Jigga sounded nonchalant all the way. "Catch me before I get someone to catch you! While you're dodging death I'ma be on a yacht, sipping some wine, fucking a model bitch!" he said and ended the call.

Knock! Knock! Knock! The maid knocked on Dolo's window, making his heart jump out of his chest. He rolled the window down; she handed him a piece of paper and walked off. Dolo read it. It was a paternity test saying that Soloman Antonio Armsted was 99.999% the father of Sean Mallory. Dolo balled the paper and threw it in the passenger seat.

"Where you at?" Dolo asked Oshun.

"Chilling, what's up?"

"I got a hella lick for your people. Send some of your people to this address." Dolo relayed the address to her.

"Okay I'm coming. And I found out who it was that brought that bounty to Face."

"Who?" Dolo had a feeling he already knew who she was going to say.

"Some dude named Jigga," she confirmed what Dolo was thinking.

"A'ight. Don't bring your ass out neither, let them handle it. Tell them when they done ransacking it, to burn that motherfucking place down. Also, you know the soul food restaurant, *Soul City*? Burn them motherfucker down too."

Dolo was going at Jigga the same way he was going to Abu. Jigga had showed him that there was no love between the two. Since he loved money so much, Dolo was going to see how felt about really losing it.

"What do you have going on?" Oshun inquired

"Some personal shit. Oh yea, I'ma get you the addresses to some more trap spots. I want you to rob them, burn them and don't leave any witnesses." Dolo orchestrated how he wanted the show to go.

"Okay and what do you want from them?"

"Nothing. I'll call you back," he pressed the end button and called Sade while getting back out of the car

"What up, bro?" she answered.

"Put me on speakerphone real quick," Dolo told her.

"You're on, now what's up?"

"Sasha, Simba, come!" He heard their nails on the wood floor. "Go watch!" Dolo heard them scramble off.

"Sean, what the hell do you have going on?"

"Listen to me good. Jigga is on some bullshit! He was playing both sides of the fence. So now I'm going at him too and he knows a lot about me, like where I stay, for instance. That's why I sent Simba and Sasha to stay outside and guard the yard. You and Samantha keep your eyes on those cameras. If need be, you can lock the house down. I'll be there shortly."

"Okay, be safe." She ended the call.

Dolo rang the doorbell as five cars drove up the driveway. Clara opened the door and Dolo put a hollow point through her forehead.

"Whatever you find is yours," Dolo told the TNT members before getting in his car and going home.

Chapter 31

Jigga struck back the next day! But he hit in an unexpected way. He killed Ms. Shannon and burned her house down. Melissa was inconsolable; she went crazy! TNT had burned down three of Jigga's restaurants but the fourth one—Melissa beat them to the punch; she went inside, killed everybody and set it on fire. Then she went to Lyncare Nursing Home and kidnapped Jigga's mom. Dolo didn't even know Jigga's mom was still alive.

"Melissa, where are you?" Dolo called her.

"I'm in the middle of something," she said, out of breath.

"What are you doing, woman?"

"Come to my apartment," she hung up.

"I'll be back!" Dolo yelled.

"Where are you going?" Samantha questioned.

"To holla at Melissa right quick."

"Be safe," she said as he was walking out the door.

Dolo pulled up to Melissa's apartment twenty minutes later. After her mom's place was burnt down, she got an apartment off of Skibo Road. Melissa answered the door in her bra and panties.

Dolo could smell the blood the instant he crossed the doorway.

He narrowed his eyes. "What's up?"

"Not shit really, the usual bullshit. Taking Jigga through it!" Melissa said nonchalantly.

"How?"

"Come on, let me show you." She walked down the hall.

The closer they got to the end of the hallway, the stronger the smell of blood was. She opened the bedroom door and Dolo shook his head. The room was covered in blood! There were body parts scattered all over the room. Dolo saw a leg by the window, an arm in the corner, a hand against the wall and a foot leaning against the closet. Dolo was trying to find out who the parts belonged to. Then, he saw the head on top of the clothes dresser. It was an old woman with a head of grey hair: Jigga's mom.

"Damn, Melissa!

"Don't tell him yet. I'm going to try and get him to trade for her."

"Does he love her?" he asked.

"More than anybody else. He would give her the world if she asked for it. I've been fucking with him for a while now so I know too much about him. That's why I don't understand why he chose to do that to my mom," her eyes watered.

"We gon' make him pay, believe that!" he consoled her. Dolo sat with Melissa in the living room until she dozed off. He slid from up under her and called Jigga.

"How good it feels to be in a position of power! In case you haven't been informed, I have your mother. Now you can save her life and lose yours or I can kill you both."

"Pussy nigga! She lived her life, kill her. I don't give a fuck! All I give a fuck about is me!" he boasted and hung up.

Damn, Dolo thought. Jigga was more treacherous than he thought. It was what it was. Dolo was just going to have to catch Jigga lacking.

***

"So what's your plan now?" Ogun asked Dolo.

"A plan? I don't have one. They've both gone off the radar. And they have enough money to stay off the grid for as long as they want."

"You need to do something to flush them out and make them show their faces," Face said, looking across his desk. Ogun, Dolo, Oshun and Face were at a club Face had just opened called *Uptown*. Dolo had told Face about Jigga trying to get him to kill him for five mil. Then, in turn, Face told Dolo that Jigga was the one who had set up the robbery at Ms. Shannon's. All Dolo could do was shake his head. Jigga had been living foul for a while.

"I was trying to flush them out with all the blowing their shit up and killing their family but they won't bite. So now I'm waiting on them to put their head out of the ground so I can chop it off."

"Basically, you're playing defense to play offense," Oshun chimed in.

"That strategy is only as good as your defense because if their offense is better than your defense, then you are a dead man. Plus, you know that neither Jigga or Abu is going to be there to attack you. They are going to sit back in the comforts of their homes and push buttons!" Face stated.

"You know what? That gives me an idea." Dolo stood up. "I'll catch up to y'all later." Dolo walked out of the club and called Sade.

"What's up, Sean?" she answered.

"Does Abu own a yacht?"

"Two of them. One of them he keeps in Miami and the other one—"

"Nah, that's all I needed to know. Tell Samantha to pack a bag. We're about to take a trip."

"What is going on?" Sade questioned.

"Jigga said something about while I'm dodging death, he was going to be on a yacht somewhere. So I'm about to see if he gave me his location without realizing it." Dolo opened his car door.

Feeling a presence behind him, Dolo spun around, leveling his Glock 30.

"Nigga, you ain't shoot nothing," Oshun teased. Dolo shook his head. "Tell Samantha to be ready when I get here." He hung up, then called Melissa. "I think I got a bead on Jigga. I'm coming to your spot after I pick up Samantha." He ended the call and addressed Oshun. "Sneaking out on me is the fastest way to the cemetery."

"Anyways," she waved him off. "So, I guess you don't need me anymore, huh?"

Dolo grabbed Oshun and picked her up and sat her on top of his car. He walked between her legs and said. "Yes, I do need you. I need you to hit some more of his traps and to be alive when I come back so I can taste this pussy." Dolo leaned down and bit Oshun's pussy through her leggings, making her grab his head and pull him up.

"Make sure you make it back and it's all yours." She stuck her tongue in his mouth.

Dolo kissed her back, causing his dick to rise up. He didn't know how it happened but he'd developed feelings for Oshun.

"A'ight, let me go." He broke the kiss.

"When you get back, you'll be proud of me."

Chapter 32

It was winter back in North Carolina, but in Miami it felt like it was springtime.

"If I had known it was going to feel like this, I would have worn some shorts," Melissa complained.

She was dressed for the winter in some black jeans and black long-sleeved shirt.

"Shut up, ain't nobody trying to hear that shit. We're down here on business, not playtime!" Dolo said, looking through the binoculars.

Dolo, Melissa and Samantha were across the store from the marina where all the pleasure crafts were. "Call Sade and ask her what is the color of the yacht again." Dolo started taking the binoculars from his face.

"Here," Samantha handed him her phone.

Dolo looked at her phone and saw a picture of a black and gray mega yacht. He should've known that the largest yacht on the water was going to be Abu's. Dolo had seen the yacht his first time scoping the marina. But he hadn't seen anyone on the deck. Dolo looked through the binoculars again and looked in the direction of the yacht.

"There he goes!" Dolo saw Jigga came up onto the deck.

Dolo followed him with the binoculars as he moved about. He watched Jigga walk to the edge of the yacht and greet Abu and Sayyid.

"We gotta get on that boat. Abu is there right now and we don't know how long of a window we have until he leaves!"

Dolo said, watching Abu until he disappeared down into the ship.

"I'm not letting him get away this time." Dolo finally put the binoculars down. "The minute the sun goes down, I'm gonna get on that boat."

Dolo estimated he had about an hour and half before the sun set and it got dark.

"I'll be back before then. I have to go get the things we're going to need for everything to go right. Y'all stay here and keep an eye on him in case he decides to leave before I get back!" Samantha told them and got out of the truck. Dolo nodded; he was in a trance. The only thing running through his mind was murder. Abu was the reason he no longer had Nah-Nah. Dolo had just met an old man with a bunch of hogs. He would feed Abu to the creatures; he despised the pig.

"You're not about to have all the fun either. Jigga has to feel me. I want my face to be the last one he sees when he takes his last breath." Melissa's face darkened.

They both had lost someone that they truly loved in the past few weeks, and those responsible were on a boat in front of them. Dolo and Melissa were both thinking of what they were going to do to their victims. Tapping on the back window got their attention, bringing them back to the present. Dolo unlocked the door and let Samantha in. He turned around and she was opening a large duffle bag.

"We're going to have to do this with a little stealth. To go in guns blazing would have the Miami PD here in minutes. So, I got us all ARP's with suppressors. I just need to know what the plan is once we get on the boat." Samantha handed Dolo and Melissa an ARP and a lightweight vest.

"After Melissa kills Jigga, we're taking Abu back with us—I have a special treat for him," Dolo said.

They waited until it was completely dark before they made their move. It turned out to be easier than they thought. They were able to just walk onto marina without anyone giving him a second glance. Dolo was the first one on the boat. The instant his feet touched the yacht's deck, an Arab appeared. Dolo shot him twice in the chest, causing him to stumble and fall overboard. The suppressor on the ARP made the gun sound like a muffled cough. They descended down the stairs single file to the lower deck, where four Arabs were lounging around playing cards. Samantha and Melissa's ARP's coughed simultaneously, sending death their way.

"We need to split up," Samantha said. "This ship is too big and I know y'all don't wanna allow them to get away."

"Okay." Dolo dashed down a hall. Dolo cleared a lower floor, and there was no sign of Abu or Jigga. He went deeper into the boat and was coming around a bend when he heard one of the ARP's cough. Dolo ran towards the sound of the gun and there stood Jigga. But he had Melissa in front of him with a gun to her head.

"Congratulations, son, you found me. But now what? You gon' kill me and risk killing her?" Jigga looked at Dolo from behind Melissa.

"Dolo," Melissa said with tears in her eyes. "He killed my mom. Kill him even if you have to kill me. As long as he dies, I'll rest easy. I'm ready to go see my mama anyway."

Dolo wasn't going to kill Melissa. He was about to tell Jigga to just take his medicine and die like a G but before Dolo could get it out of his mouth, Melissa grabbed Jigga's gun hand and squeezed the trigger, blowing half her face off. The only feature left on her face was her lip. Her body fell leaving Jigga open to feel Dolo's wrath. *Kah! Kah!* Dolo emptied the clip into Jigga. Every time one of the .223 entered him, his body would jerk. It looked like he was doing a Harlem shake. Dolo looked at Jigga's body one last time and walked out.

"Dolo! I got him!" Samantha screamed. Dolo rushed to the sound of the voice. When he finally made it to her, she had Abu at gunpoint. They were forced to look around the room. The floor had a beige carpet that your feet sunk into. The walls were a dark blue with gold rimming and borders. There were regal George Catlin portraits of Indians and Russell watercolors of cowboys on the walls. The chandelier was pure gold. There was a hot tub towards the bathroom. Then his eyes landed back on Abu.

"Damn, Abu you don't know how good that makes me feel! I've dreamed about this day every day for the last few months." Dolo paused, staring Abu in the eyes.

Even though Dolo clearly had the upper hand, Abu sat on the sofa with his legs crossed, staring at Dolo with a sly smirk on his face.

"I want you to have the same smirk on your face when I throw you in the hog pen."

"I got two hundred million for my life. If you let me live, I'll wire each of you a hundred million dollars," Abu said nonchalantly as if he was giving away a few dollars.

"Maybe next time." Dolo slapped him with the ARP, knocking him out.

Chapter 33

When Abu woke up, his hands were tied behind his back and his mouth had a rag in it. His being bound wasn't as unnerving as the animal growls he heard. Abu rolled over his side and saw a pen full of the biggest pigs he'd ever seen in his life.

"Good you're awake just in time for feeding," Dolo said, squatting down in front of Abu.

"Mmm, mmm!" Abu mumbled through the rag.

"I honestly don't give a fuck what you have to say because nothing you can say will save your life."

"Let 'em talk, they'll be the last words he'll ever say anyway?" John Doe drawled.

They were far out in the county; they were so deep in the woods that the county sheriffs didn't even come out here. Dolo had met John Doe at a chicken fight. They got to talking about dogs and clicked. That's when Dolo found out about what he does. John Doe was a real bonafide country boy. He stood 6'7" and was every bit of four hundred pounds. He sported an afro that looked like it had never seen a comb. He was dark-skinned, with bushy eyebrows, close set eyes, broad nose and small pink lips. And no matter the weather, he always wore overalls. Dolo shook his head and snatched the rag out of Abu's mouth.

"Your grandmother isn't dead. I still have her. If you let me go, I'll release her." Abu rushed his words out.

Pow! Dolo punched him in the mouth.

"Call whoever is holding her and have them release her immediately." Dolo said through gritted teeth.

"Give me your phone," Abu said, holding his jaw.

"And speak English, motherfucker," Dolo said, handing him his phone.

"Sayyid, take the old woman downtown and drop her off. Do it now!" he said and hung up.

Dolo grabbed the phone and called Sade.

"Yo, Nah-Nah is about to be downtown somewhere. I need you to get her asap and call me when you get her." Dolo ended the call.

"If you think for one minute that having her let go is going to save you, it's not. Your reign of terror has come to an end. I'm going to enjoy watching the pigs devour you. And they haven't been fed in a week, so they're starving." Dolo smiled sadistically.

Once Abu was dead, Dolo was going to take a much needed break.

"I thought you were going to let me go once you got her back," Abu said, confused.

"Let's go ahead and put him in there with his hogs." Samantha walked into the barn, carrying a M16.

"Once Sade grabs Nah-Nah, he's going in the pen."

"Nah-Nah?"

"Yes. The pussy had her the whole time. He just told Sayyid to drop her off downtown. When Sade calls and tells me she has her, I'ma record the hogs eating him alive."

"I can't believe you consider yourself a gangster but you're putting yourself through all of this for a Fed," Abu spat.

"Sade isn't a fed, first off. Secondly, she's my little sister!" Dolo defended her

"She had you fooled. She's working with the feds to try and take me down."

"I already know what's going on," Dolo said before answering his phone. "What's up, Sade?"

"I have her!" Sade said excitedly.

"Bet. Take her to the house," Dolo said, hanging up. "Time to go meet Allah," Dolo said, getting ready to grab Abu.

"Wait, wait, wait!" Abu yelled.

"He's stalling. My hogs are hungry!" John Doe drawled.

"Ha-Ha! Ha-Ha! Ha, ha, ha, ha!" Abu started laughing real hard, catching everybody off guard. Dolo, Samantha and John Doe all looked at each other.

"What the fuck are you laughing at, fuck nigga?" Dolo questioned.

"At you, dummy!" He spat at Dolo's feet. "It's clear you really don't know who I am or how my father is, but you're soon to find out. Matter of fact, you'll probably find out in the next few minutes. Allowing me to use your phone was your worst mistake. They're going to track your phone to this location!" Abu said and then Dolo heard what sounded like a helicopter.

"What in Sam's hell is dat noise dere?" John Doe walked out of the barn to see what the noise was.

No sooner had he crossed the opening of the barn door than it sounded like a cannon was being shot. All Dolo saw was John Doe's body split in half.

"Shit!" Dolo said, jumping up to his feet and started pushing them to the back of the barn.

"Hurry up!" Samantha yelled.

Kah! Kah! Kah! Sayyid walked in the doorway shooting a fully automatic Micro Uzi Pro. Then he stopped because he couldn't risk shooting Abu. Samantha pointed the M16 Sayyid's way and let off, making him dive for cover. Dolo looked out the front and saw about thirty Arabs advancing towards the barn.

"You'll be dead soon." Abu threatened.

"Shut up!" Samantha hit him in the mouth with the Uzi, knocking some of his teeth out.

Dolo shot all the lights out, bathing the barn in darkness. Then, he went over and unlocked the hog pen just as all the Arabs came into the barn. The big hogs rushed towards the door. By the time the Arabs knew what was going on, the hogs were on them. Dolo pushed Abu out the back of the barn, leaving behind the gunshots and screams of the unsuspecting Arabs. Dolo stepped out the back and saw stars. Sayyid brought his gun down on Dolo's head, causing him to stumble.

La! La! La! Samantha's M16 started chanting, taking the top of Sayyid's head off. Dolo got to his feet and heard Abu scream. Dolo looked and saw a hog had bit his leg, causing him to fall to the ground. Abu's life was over after that because a two-hundred-pound hog came up and bit Abu in the face, leaving nothing but a hole where his eye, nose and mouth used to be. Dolo and Samantha disappeared into the night.

Epilogue

Three months after Abu's death, everything went back to normal. Nah-Nah was back at Heavenly Comforts. Samantha moved to Fayetteville to be closer to Dolo and Sade. Sade moved out of Dolo's house and had got her own spot. Dolo and Oshun were in a relationship, with a baby on the way.

"Girl, you are silly as hell!" Sade told Oshun.

"I'm just saying ain't that right, baby?" Oshun asked Dolo.

"Yea," he said, looking out the window into his yard.

"What's wrong with you?" Oshun could tell when something wasn't right with Dolo.

Dolo shook his head and walked in the back.

"What's wrong with him, girl?" Sade inquired.

"I have no clue."

"Baby! What's up?" Oshun asked as Dolo came back in the living room with his gun in one hand and some papers in the other ones.

"I've been asking myself for the last month what I was going to do about you, Sade, and I couldn't make my mind up."

"What are you talking about, bro?" Sade asked.

"Don't *bro* me, special agent Sade Christina Richards!" Dolo said, and she dropped her head.

"Special Agent?" Oshun got up and walked over and stood by Dolo"

"When we had Abu in the barn, he said Sade was a FED and that she had me fooled but I brushed it off. But it was nagging at me, so I started digging. Lo and behold! Sade really is the FBI but it gets deeper than that, doesn't it, Sade?" Dolo handed Oshun the papers in his hand.

"Wow!" Oshun read the papers and pulled one of her knives out.

"I bet you know what these papers are, Sade. See, before me and Jigga fell out, I was telling him that you are my sister and he said my mom told him that you were a stillborn. Sure enough, the papers say that my real baby sister was stillborn. So who are you?" Dolo gripped his gun tightly.

Sade looked up with tears in her eyes and said: "To be honest, I was sent to gather intel on Abu and Jigga so that we could put them in prison for eternity. Then your name came up and my superior put that above them because your name popped up as the number one hit man in the U.S. They gave me the background to use and I did it. All this happened after you saved me and Chadijah's life. After that, I couldn't and wasn't going to give them any information on you," Sade confessed.

"You're a federal agent?" Samantha walked in on the conversation.

"Once the law is always the law!" Oshun said and the three of them ended Sade's life with two bullets and a knife.

THE END

Lock Down Publications and Ca$h Presents
Assisted Publishing Packages

BASIC PACKAGE	UPGRADED PACKAGE
$499 Editing Cover Design Formatting	$800 Typing Editing Cover Design Formatting
ADVANCE PACKAGE $1,200 Typing Editing Cover Design Formatting Copyright registration Proofreading Upload book to Amazon	**LDP SUPREME PACKAGE** $1,500 Typing Editing Cover Design Formatting Copyright registration Proofreading Set up Amazon account Upload book to Amazon Advertise on LDP, Amazon and Facebook Page

***Other services available upon request.
Additional charges may apply

Lock Down Publications
P.O. Box 944
Stockbridge, GA 30281-9998
Phone: 470 303-9761

Submission Guideline

Submit the first three chapters of your completed manuscript to ldpsubmissions@gmail.com. In the subject line add **Your Book's Title**. The manuscript must be in a Word Doc file and sent as an attachment. Document should be in Times New Roman, double spaced, and in size 12 font. Also, provide your synopsis and full contact information. If sending multiple submissions, they must each be in a separate email.

Have a story but no way to send it electronically? You can still submit to LDP/Ca$h Presents. Send in the first three chapters, written or typed, of your completed manuscript to:

LDP: Submissions Dept
P.O. Box 944
Stockbridge, GA 30281-9998

DO NOT send original manuscript. Must be a duplicate. Provide your synopsis and a cover letter containing your full contact information.

Thanks for considering LDP and Ca$h Presents.

NEW RELEASES

BLOODLINE OF A SAVAGE 1&2
THESE VICIOUS STREETS
RELENTLESS GOON
RELENTLESS GOON 2
BY PRINCE A. TAUHID

THE BUTTERFLY MAFIA 1-3
BY FUMIYA PAYNE

A THUG'S STREET PRINCESS 1&2
BY MEESHA

CITY OF SMOKE 2
BY MOLOTTI

STEPPERS 1,2&3
BY KING RIO

THE LANE 1&2
BY KEN-KEN SPENCE

THUG OF SPADES 1&2
LOVE IN THE TRENCHES 2
BY COREY ROBINSON

TIL DEATH 3
BY ARYANNA

THE BIRTH OF A GANGSTER 4
BY DELMONT PLAYER

PRODUCT OF THE STREETS 1&2
BY DEMOND "MONEY" ANDERSON

NO TIME FOR ERROR
BY KEESE

MONEY HUNGRY DEMONS
BY TRANAY ADAMS

Coming Soon from Lock Down Publications/Ca$h Presents

IF YOU CROSS ME ONCE 6
ANGEL V
By Anthony Fields

IMMA DIE BOUT MINE 4&5
By Aryanna

A THUGS STREET PRINCESS 3
By Meesha

PRODUCT OF THE STREETS 3
By Demond Money Anderson

CORNER BOYS
By Corey Robinson

SON OF A DOPE FIEND 4
By Renta

THE MURDER QUEENS 6&7
By Michael Gallon

CITY OF SMOKE 3
By Molotti

BETRAYAL OF A G
By Ray Vinci

CONFESSIONS OF A DOPE BOY
By Nicholas Lock

THA TAKEOVER
By Keith Chandler

Available Now

RESTRAINING ORDER 1 & 2
By **CA$H & Coffee**

LOVE KNOWS NO BOUNDARIES 1-3
By **Coffee**

RAISED AS A GOON I, II, III & IV
BRED BY THE SLUMS I, II, III
BLAST FOR ME I & II
ROTTEN TO THE CORE I II III
A BRONX TALE I, II, III
DUFFLE BAG CARTEL I II III IV V VI
HEARTLESS GOON I II III IV V
A SAVAGE DOPEBOY I II
DRUG LORDS I II III
CUTTHROAT MAFIA I II
KING OF THE TRENCHES
By **Ghost**

LAY IT DOWN I & II
LAST OF A DYING BREED I II
BLOOD STAINS OF A SHOTTA I & II III
By **Jamaica**

LOYAL TO THE GAME I II III
LIFE OF SIN I, II III
By **TJ & Jelissa**

IF LOVING HIM IS WRONG…I & II
LOVE ME EVEN WHEN IT HURTS I II III
By **Jelissa**

BLOODY COMMAS I & II
SKI MASK CARTEL I, II & III
KING OF NEW YORK I II, III IV V
RISE TO POWER I II III
COKE KINGS I II III IV V
BORN HEARTLESS I II III IV
KING OF THE TRAP I II
By **T.J. Edwards**

WHEN THE STREETS CLAP BACK I & II III
THE HEART OF A SAVAGE I II III IV
MONEY MAFIA I II
LOYAL TO THE SOIL I II III
By **Jibril Williams**

A DISTINGUISHED THUG STOLE MY HEART I II &
III
LOVE SHOULDN'T HURT I II III IV
RENEGADE BOYS 1-4
PAID IN KARMA 1-3
SAVAGE STORMS 1-3
AN UNFORESEEN LOVE 1-3
BABY, I'M WINTERTIME COLD 1-3
A THUG'S STREET PRINCESS 1&2
By **Meesha**

A GANGSTER'S CODE 1-3
A GANGSTER'S SYN 1-3
THE SAVAGE LIFE 1-3
CHAINED TO THE STREETS 1-3
BLOOD ON THE MONEY 1-3
A GANGSTA'S PAIN 1-3
BEAUTIFUL LIES AND UGLY TRUTHS
CHURCH IN THESE STREETS
By **J-Blunt**

PUSH IT TO THE LIMIT
By **Bre' Hayes**

BLOOD OF A BOSS 1-5
SHADOWS OF THE GAME
TRAP BASTARD
By **Askari**

THE STREETS BLEED MURDER 1-3
THE HEART OF A GANGSTA 1-3
By **Jerry Jackson**

CUM FOR ME 1-8
An LDP Erotica Collaboration

BRIDE OF A HUSTLA 1-3
THE FETTI GIRLS 1-3
CORRUPTED BY A GANGSTA 1-4
BLINDED BY HIS LOVE
THE PRICE YOU PAY FOR LOVE 1-3
DOPE GIRL MAGIC 1-3
By **Destiny Skai**

WHEN A GOOD GIRL GOES BAD
By **Adrienne**

A KINGPIN'S AMBITION
A KINGPIN'S AMBITION II
I MURDER FOR THE DOUGH
By **Ambitious**

THE COST OF LOYALTY 1-3
By **Kweli**

A GANGSTER'S REVENGE 1-4
THE BOSS MAN'S DAUGHTERS 1-5
A SAVAGE LOVE 1&2
BAE BELONGS TO ME 1&2
A HUSTLER'S DECEIT 1-3
WHAT BAD BITCHES DO 1-3
SOUL OF A MONSTER 1-3
KILL ZONE
A DOPE BOY'S QUEEN 1-3
TIL DEATH 1-3
IMMA DIE BOUT MINE 1-3
By **Aryanna**

TRUE SAVAGE 1-7
DOPE BOY MAGIC 1-3
MIDNIGHT CARTEL 1-3
CITY OF KINGZ 1&2
NIGHTMARE ON SILENT AVE
THE PLUG OF LIL MEXICO 1&2
CLASSIC CITY
By **Chris Green**

A DOPEBOY'S PRAYER
By **Eddie "Wolf" Lee**

THE KING CARTEL 1-3
By **Frank Gresham**

THESE NIGGAS AIN'T LOYAL 1-3
By **Nikki Tee**

GANGSTA SHYT 1-3
By **CATO**

THE ULTIMATE BETRAYAL
By **Phoenix**

BOSS'N UP 1-3
By **Royal Nicole**

I LOVE YOU TO DEATH
By **Destiny J**

I RIDE FOR MY HITTA
I STILL RIDE FOR MY HITTA
By **Misty Holt**

LOVE & CHASIN' PAPER
By **Qay Crockett**

TO DIE IN VAIN
SINS OF A HUSTLA
By **ASAD**

BROOKLYN HUSTLAZ
By **Boogsy Morina**

BROOKLYN ON LOCK 1 & 2
By **Sonovia**

GANGSTA CITY
By **Teddy Duke**

A DRUG KING AND HIS DIAMOND 1-3
A DOPEMAN'S RICHES
HER MAN, MINE'S TOO 1&2
CASH MONEY HO'S
THE WIFEY I USED TO BE 1&2
PRETTY GIRLS DO NASTY THINGS
By **Nicole Goosby**

LIPSTICK KILLAH 1-3
CRIME OF PASSION 1-3
FRIEND OR FOE 1-3
By **Mimi**

TRAPHOUSE KING 1-3
KINGPIN KILLAZ 1-3
STREET KINGS 1&2
PAID IN BLOOD 1&2
CARTEL KILLAZ 1-3
DOPE GODS 1&2
By **Hood Rich**

STEADY MOBBN' 1-3
THE STREETS STAINED MY SOUL 1-3
By **Marcellus Allen**

WHO SHOT YA 1-3
SON OF A DOPE FIEND 1-3
HEAVEN GOT A GHETTO 1&2
SKI MASK MONEY 1&2
By **Renta**

GORILLAZ IN THE BAY 1-4
TEARS OF A GANGSTA 1/&2
3X KRAZY 1&2
STRAIGHT BEAST MODE 1&2
By **DE'KARI**

TRIGGADALE 1-3
MURDA WAS THE CASE 1-3
By **Elijah R. Freeman**

THE STREETS ARE CALLING
By **Duquie Wilson**

SLAUGHTER GANG 1-3
RUTHLESS HEART 1-3
By **Willie Slaughter**

GOD BLESS THE TRAPPERS 1-3
THESE SCANDALOUS STREETS 1-3
FEAR MY GANGSTA 1-5
THESE STREETS DON'T LOVE NOBODY 1-2
BURY ME A G 1-5
A GANGSTA'S EMPIRE 1-4
THE DOPEMAN'S BODYGAURD 1&2
THE REALEST KILLAZ 1-3
THE LAST OF THE OGS 1-3
By **Tranay Adams**

MARRIED TO A BOSS 1-3
By **Destiny Skai & Chris Green**

KINGZ OF THE GAME 1-7
CRIME BOSS 1-3
By **Playa Ray**

FUK SHYT
By **Blakk Diamond**

DON'T F#CK WITH MY HEART 1&2
By **Linnea**

ADDICTED TO THE DRAMA 1-3
IN THE ARM OF HIS BOSS
By **Jamila**

LOYALTY AIN'T PROMISED 1&2
By **Keith Williams**

YAYO 1-4
A SHOOTER'S AMBITION 1&2
BRED IN THE GAME
By **S. Allen**

TRAP GOD 1-3
RICH $AVAGE 1-3
MONEY IN THE GRAVE 1-3
CARTEL MONEY
By **Martell Troublesome Bolden**

FOREVER GANGSTA 1&2
GLOCKS ON SATIN SHEETS 1&2
By **Adrian Dulan**

TOE TAGZ 1-4
LEVELS TO THIS SHYT 1&2
IT'S JUST ME AND YOU
By **Ah'Million**

KINGPIN DREAMS 1-3
RAN OFF ON DA PLUG
By **Paper Boi Rari**

CONFESSIONS OF A GANGSTA 1-4
CONFESSIONS OF A JACKBOY 1-3
CONFESSIONS OF A HITMAN
By **Nicholas Lock**

I'M NOTHING WITHOUT HIS LOVE
SINS OF A THUG
TO THE THUG I LOVED BEFORE
A GANGSTA SAVED XMAS
IN A HUSTLER I TRUST
By **Monet Dragun**

QUIET MONEY 1-3
THUG LIFE 1-3
EXTENDED CLIP 1&2
A GANGSTA'S PARADISE
By **Trai'Quan**

CAUGHT UP IN THE LIFE 1-3
THE STREETS NEVER LET GO 1-3
By **Robert Baptiste**

NEW TO THE GAME 1-3
MONEY, MURDER & MEMORIES 1-3
By **Malik D. Rice**

CREAM 2-3
THE STREETS WILL TALK
By **Yolanda Moore**

LIFE OF A SAVAGE 1-4
A GANGSTA'S QUR'AN 1-4
MURDA SEASON 1-3
GANGLAND CARTEL 1-3
CHI'RAQ GANGSTAS 1-4
KILLERS ON ELM STREET 1-3
JACK BOYZ N DA BRONX 1-3
A DOPEBOY'S DREAM 1-3
JACK BOYS VS DOPE BOYS 1-3
COKE GIRLZ
COKE BOYS
SOSA GANG 1&2
BRONX SAVAGES
BODYMORE KINGPINS
BLOOD OF A GOON
By **Romell Tukes**

THE STREETS MADE ME 1-3
By **Larry D. Wright**

CONCRETE KILLA 1-3
VICIOUS LOYALTY 1-3
By **Kingpen**

THE ULTIMATE SACRIFICE 1-6
KHADIFI
IF YOU CROSS ME ONCE 1-3
ANGEL 1-4
IN THE BLINK OF AN EYE
By **Anthony Fields**

THE LIFE OF A HOOD STAR
By **Ca$h & Rashia Wilson**

THE STREETS WILL NEVER CLOSE 1-3
By **K'ajji**

NIGHTMARES OF A HUSTLA 1-3
By **King Dream**

HARD AND RUTHLESS 1&2
MOB TOWN 251
THE BILLIONAIRE BENTLEYS 1-3
REAL G'S MOVE IN SILENCE
By **Von Diesel**

GHOST MOB
By **Stilloan Robinson**

MOB TIES 1-6
SOUL OF A HUSTLER, HEART OF A KILLER 1-3
GORILLAZ IN THE TRENCHES
By **SayNoMore**

BODYMORE MURDERLAND 1-3
THE BIRTH OF A GANGSTER 1-4
By **Delmont Player**

FOR THE LOVE OF A BOSS 1&2
By **C. D. Blue**

KILLA KOUNTY 1-5
By **Khufu**

MOBBED UP 1-4
THE BRICK MAN 1-5
THE COCAINE PRINCESS 1-10
STEPPERS 1-3
SUPER GREMLIN 1-4
By **King Rio**

MONEY GAME 1&2
By **Smoove Dolla**

A GANGSTA'S KARMA 1-4
By **FLAME**

KING OF THE TRENCHES 1-3
By **GHOST & TRANAY ADAMS**

QUEEN OF THE ZOO 1&2
By **Black Migo**

GRIMEY WAYS 1-3
By **Ray Vinci**

XMAS WITH AN ATL SHOOTER
By **Ca$h & Destiny Skai**

CONFESSIONS OF A HITMAN | NICHOLAS LOCK

KING KILLA 1&2
By **Vincent "Vitto" Holloway**

BETRAYAL OF A THUG 1&2
By **Fre$h**

THE MURDER QUEENS 1-5
By **Michael Gallon**

FOR THE LOVE OF BLOOD 1-4
By **Jamel Mitchell**

HOOD CONSIGLIERE 1&2
NO TIME FOR ERROR
By **Keese**

PROTÉGÉ OF A LEGEND 1&2
LOVE IN THE TRENCHES 1&2
By **Corey Robinson**

BORN IN THE GRAVE 1-3
CRIME PAYS
By **Self Made Tay**

MOAN IN MY MOUTH
By **XTASY**

TORN BETWEEN A GANGSTER AND A GENTLEMAN
By **J-BLUNT & Miss Kim**

LOYALTY IS EVERYTHING 1-3
CITY OF SMOKE 1&2
By **Molotti**

HERE TODAY GONE TOMORROW 1&2
By **Fly Rock**

WOMEN LIE MEN LIE 1-4
FIFTY SHADES OF SNOW 1-3
STACK BEFORE YOU SPLURGE
GIRLS FALL LIKE DOMINOES
NAÏVE TO THE STREETS
By **ROY MILLIGAN**

PILLOW PRINCESS
By **S. Hawkins**

THE BUTTERFLY MAFIA 1-3
SALUTE MY SAVAGERY 1&2
By **Fumiya Payne**

THE LANE 1&2
By Ken-Ken Spence

THE PUSSY TRAP 1-5
By **Nene Capri**

DIRTY DNA
By **Blaque**

SANCTIFIED AND HORNY
by **XTASY**

BOOKS BY LDP'S CEO, CA$H

TRUST IN NO MAN
TRUST IN NO MAN 2
TRUST IN NO MAN 3
BONDED BY BLOOD
SHORTY GOT A THUG
THUGS CRY
THUGS CRY 2
THUGS CRY 3
TRUST NO BITCH
TRUST NO BITCH 2
TRUST NO BITCH 3
TIL MY CASKET DROPS
RESTRAINING ORDER
RESTRAINING ORDER 2
IN LOVE WITH A CONVICT
LIFE OF A HOOD STAR
XMAS WITH AN ATL SHOOTER